LOVING

Lily

Jennifer Smith Widmer

ISBN 978-1-63630-810-4 (Paperback)
ISBN 978-1-63630-811-1 (Digital)

Covenant Books, Inc.
11661 Hwy 707
Murrells Inlet, SC 29576
www.covenantbooks.com

With much love to all the ones I love

PROLOGUE

Ammon closed his eyes and took a deep breath of the cold, misty air. He framed the picture in his mind and then, while opening his eyes, slowly raised his camera to capture another image of the magnificent view.

Dunnottar Castle had been raised upon a rocky headland that jutted out into the boisterous North Sea about three kilometers south of Stonehaven in Aberdeenshire, Scotland. To him, it was the epitome of a medieval castle with its strong keep, surrounding buildings and battlements, and the ocean protecting it from invasion on three sides.

The ruins of this fortress melded so well with the surrounding cliffs that the castle looked almost carved from the stones themselves, further enhancing the feeling of timelessness. The entire place seemed to transport him back in time. For a moment, he thought he could hear an ancient drum and trumpet calling him to battle against an invading foe. It was a heady feeling, standing amidst such history and feeling a part of it.

Coming back to the present with a slight shiver, Ammon pulled his coat a little tighter around himself. The early April air had a lingering bite of winter that was sharpening with the soon-to-be setting sun. Scotland, especially along its coast, was famous for its cold weather, and Ammon was grateful for the heavy wool coat he currently wore. He watched other tourists wandering about the grounds and noticed that some were less prepared for the chill of the ocean winds and the persistent dampness associated with the sea. He heard the pounding of the waves 160 feet below him and was grateful for the protection of the cliffs that kept some of that moisture at bay.

He let his eyes wander again across the buildings and grounds, looking for the perfect place to capture the images he had in his mind. As a photographer for a prominent natural history magazine, he had spent many such hours observing and cultivating a project before he ever started snapping pictures. Even in this age of digital photography, Ammon still loved the idea of capturing an image with his mind and eyes before he committed it to the camera.

This was his third trip to the castle. His first visit was four years ago, and he had come on a work assignment to capture images of castles throughout Scotland. While here, he had fallen in love with this particular area.

His second visit two years ago happened during a rainy period of days. While the weather had matched his mood at that time, it had not afforded him the possibility of capturing a beautiful sun setting behind the keep. That was the shot he had wanted since his first visit, and it prompted him to stop here again while he was in the country.

Only six months had passed before this third visit, and the weather couldn't be more different. With today's gorgeous clear blue skies that held on to a few wispy clouds, his hopes for several stunning silhouettes of the castle seemed guaranteed.

With another look around him, Ammon noticed most of the visitors beginning to head toward the gatehouse and the footpath that would take them back down the cliffs and onto the mainland. He had been given special permission to stay past the castle's closing for his shots, and he looked forward to the quiet that descended as the chattering groups of tourists faded away.

Ammon stooped down to pick up his camera bags and gather his supplies. His plan was to walk from his current position near the stables to the old sentry box that sat farthest southeast of all the old fortifications. From there, he would slowly walk up toward the chapel and the keep, following the sun as it sets behind the buildings. He was only half paying attention to the lingering tourists as he stood up, but then his eyes caught hold of an image that immediately captured his attention.

Gazing at her profile, he could see her eyes watching the sea. Somehow, he knew she was consuming the sight of the ocean waves coming toward the castle and breaking on the rocks below. Her left hand was placed on the wall of the sentry box, her body angled forward as if wishing to be able to see all the way to the bottom of the cliffs but not wanting to get too close to the edge. Her long, wavy strawberry-blond hair was blowing in the wind, pulled back by the breeze, and streaming behind her. The setting sun highlighted a calm and pensive face.

She was not a classic beauty, but the serenity she exuded made her stunning. She had on a warm woolen sweater, jeans, and short boots. Outside of the modern clothes, she looked like the daughter of a Scottish chieftain surveying her kingdom and communing with the ancient spirits of the sea.

He realized that she was alone and apparently so absorbed in her thoughts that she failed to notice that she was the last one inside the castle walls besides himself and a few workers. He slowly lowered his bags back to the ground while holding onto his camera. He took several pictures before she suddenly sensed the quiet. Turning, she walked quickly toward the gateway. He lowered his camera before she saw him and was rewarded with only a slightly interested glance as she walked past the stables on her way out.

After a moment, he gathered his belongings for a second time and finally succeeded in moving himself to his chosen location which, ironically, was right where she had been standing. He shook his head and looked at the castle again, attempting to push aside the scene he had just witnessed.

As he once again raised his camera and began taking pictures, he found he could not entirely rid himself of the one image he had not meant to capture today but which, somehow, he knew he would never be able to forget.

1
chapter

The conversation had started out innocently enough, but she really should have seen it coming. Lily Manning considered herself an introvert, but she still made an effort to get to know people, especially the new nurses in the labor unit where she worked. She struck up conversations and allowed people to talk about themselves to their hearts' content, though she rarely offered much insight into her own life outside of the hospital.

Besides sharing memories from her travels and other adventures, Lily employed a strict no-details policy about her personal life. As a rule, she particularly avoided mentioning her relationship status, which was single—100 percent single.

It's not that she didn't like the idea of dating, but whenever anyone got a whiff of her singleness, the next question out of their mouths would inevitably be "How do you feel about blind dates?" Lily had long since decided that blind dates were the most torturous form of dating known to man.

She knew that people often found relationships through matches made by their friends, but she had not been so lucky. All of her blind dating experiences just proved to her that when someone said they knew a guy that was perfect for her, what they really meant was that he was also single and this was the only qualification necessary to fall in love.

She hadn't meant to let Susan, a new employee on her unit, know that she was single. Susan had been talking about her grown and married children, and Lily, listening attentively, wasn't thinking about her own non-married status during the conversation.

Consequently, when Susan mentioned she had a single nephew who had recently moved into the area, Lily wondered aloud where he would live as there were many single people in her neighborhood. Lily caught Susan's eyes brightening and quickly realized her mistake, but it was too late.

So here she sat, on a bright mid-August morning, next to her blind date, Steve. His looks were decent enough, not so handsome that he'd be picked out of a crowd, but he wasn't terrible-looking either. He was thirty, only two years older than Lily's twenty-eight, and slightly taller too, which was a must in Lily's book.

As a mechanical engineer, Lily thought he might even be interesting to talk to, but she'd probably never know since he seemed glued to his cell phone. He had made a slight effort at some stilted conversation when they first sat down together, but when he received a text fifteen minutes into their date, he lifted up his phone to answer it and had been engrossed ever since.

Lily thought it was pathetic that people seemed unable to communicate organically anymore. Without a screen to separate them from the real world, many of her dates seemed frozen by the idea of carrying on an actual conversation. It was like peoples' mouths had stopped working, and only their fingers were capable of expressing their opinions. *Perhaps if I texted him a question, he'd converse with me,* Lily thought, laughing to herself.

She reached for her phone just as the waiter passed by and dropped off the check. Lily sighed, filled with relief that she now had an excuse to leave. Happily, they had driven separately and met at the café so all that remained now was a perfunctory goodbye, and she would be free to go.

She waited for Steve's eyes to lift from his phone and acknowledge the check, but he still seemed enamored by his screen. After a few moments, Lily's eyes narrowed. Surely, he was not completely obtuse. He had to know the check was sitting right there.

Lily shifted in her chair and coughed lightly. Still, Steve's eyes looked fixedly at his phone. Lily's eyebrow lifted as the truth dawned on her: he was deliberately ignoring the check! Did he honestly think she was going to pay for all of it? Not that she couldn't or even that she would mind doing it just to get out of here, but if he was that tight-fisted, the least he could do was ask the waiter to split the check.

Lily rolled her eyes and reached for the bill, desperate enough to leave that she decided to just put down cash for her share of the meal and go. However, at that moment, a breeze caught the check and lifted it off the table. Her small gasp of surprise performed the feat which a moment ago seemed impossible; Steve raised his eyes from his phone. He looked up just as the check fluttered past his face. He reached for it out of instinct and then realized what he held.

Lily smiled for the first time that morning. Placing a couple of bills on the table, she stood up, kindly told Steve to have a nice life, and walked quickly away to her car.

As she drove, Lily found herself shaking her head in disgust. Coming to a stop at a red light halfway home, she found she could no longer contain her frustration with her long string of disagreeable dates. "Why?" Lily cried out inside her car as she brought her forehead down on her steering wheel.

Lifting her head, the thought came again that maybe it was her. Perhaps something about her was so repulsive that not one man seemed capable of wanting to get to know her. For the life of her, she couldn't figure out what that could be, but she was running out of reasons for these continuing failures. She knew she wasn't the most amazing person on the planet, but she didn't think she was all that terrible.

Her mind ran through all the comments she'd heard throughout the years. Men referred to her as tall, intimidating, or too smart. Maybe that was the problem. Was her confidence in her abilities and her mind the opposite of what men looked for? Did her height just add to her overall lack of appeal? She'd always felt confident in every aspect of her life, except when it came to men.

Lily placed her forehead against the steering wheel again. As she did so, she noticed another car pulling up beside her at the light and its occupant looking at her with some concern. She quickly raised her head and drove the remainder of the way home quietly. Though she remained completely annoyed on the inside, she decided that she would contain the rest of her angst for the punching bags at the gym.

2
chapter

Lily concentrated on putting the disastrous blind date of that morning behind her. She went on a long run, pounded on the punching bag, and then came home and mowed her lawn. By lunchtime, she'd forgotten all about whatever-his-name-was. Instead, she was looking forward to her evening plans with her older brother.

Will was bringing his wife, Kate, over for a dinner and game night. Lily always had to laugh when she thought of the two of them. Will had endured unending teasing for marrying a woman named Kate. The popularity of the British royals made making jokes at their names a continual source of amusement in the family. In fact, Kate was most generally just called Princess by Lily's younger brother, Jack.

Thankfully, Kate was half-Hawaiian and lived up to the chillness associated with the islands. She took the teasing in stride and dished it back out with good-natured humor. Lily loved Kate and thought of her as the sister she'd never had growing up. Being raised with two brothers made her relationship with Kate special.

Thinking of Kate must have put a vibe into the cosmos because a few minutes later Lily's phone rang. "Kate! How'd you know I was thinking of you?" Lily joked as she picked up the call.

"I'm a genius," said Kate drily. "But we already knew that. Anyway, I was wondering how much trouble it would be if we brought another person along with us tonight."

Lily paused. Will and Kate knew better than to set her up, especially in her own home where she couldn't escape. Not wanting to assume the worst though, Lily said, "It would probably be okay. Who are you bringing?"

Kate hesitated for a moment and then responded, "An old roommate of Will's. Ammon Hunter." She must have heard Lily's exasperated sigh because she hurried to say, "It's not a setup, Lil. He just got back into town from a work trip, and Will told him to come over for dinner before he remembered we were coming to your house. I swear I would never try and set you up like this! It was just an honest mistake on Will's part." After a short pause, Kate said reluctantly, "We could always call him back and cancel too, if it's too much hassle."

Lily sighed once again but this time in amused defeat. Will hadn't done it on purpose, and she really didn't mind too much if it was an old friend of her brother. "He can come, Kate. Don't even worry about it. Just tell Will that he owes me one, and I don't intend to forget it."

"Done," said Kate happily. "And from what Will's told me, he has a really interesting job so he should have some fun stories to share over dinner."

Lily and Kate talked a few more minutes, and then Kate said she needed to let Will know the plan. Lily laughed to herself after getting off the phone. Will could have called himself, but he knew Kate had the better chance of succeeding in getting Lily to agree to the change in dinner plans.

Lily set her phone down and walked toward the bathroom. After all her running around this morning, a shower was definitely in order. And it wouldn't hurt to take a little extra time getting ready. Just in case.

3
chapter

Ammon went through the motions of getting ready for dinner, but his mind wasn't on the evening ahead. His thoughts slipped into the past as he rummaged through his suitcase looking for a clean set of clothes.

He had recently returned to the area after several long work assignments. The slight clutter of his hotel room showed evidence of his exhausted state; he usually kept things more organized. Soon enough, though, he'd be moving into an actual apartment, and the mess would be contained.

Truthfully, he could afford to buy a nice home if he wanted to. His job paid well, and he had always been wise with his money. Financially speaking, purchasing a home was likely smarter than continuing to rent. But a home meant permanence, and he still wasn't sold on the idea of living in the west. Part of him still missed living near his family in Binghamton, New York. Plus, owning a house made him think about having a family of his own, and the possibility of that happening seemed remote.

Ammon found the clothes he wanted to wear and slipped them on. As he walked to the bathroom, his eyes caught sight of the small framed picture sitting on the desk near his bed. This picture of Dunnottar Castle showed grounds wet with rain, moss-streaked rock walls glistening with captured moisture, and a dark and cloudy sky.

He'd gone back to the castle two years ago, right after his relationship with Laura had failed. He'd felt completely blindsided by her betrayal, and he'd run away to Scotland to try and figure out his life. The rain hadn't stopped his entire visit, and he remembered sitting on the grounds of the castle, drenched and wondering why he had ever allowed himself to feel in the first place.

He didn't know what had caused Laura to leave him for another man, but he figured that something about him hadn't been enough. Maybe he didn't know how to love her like he should. Perhaps he wasn't appealing enough in his thoughts or his dreams for the future. Whatever it was, she'd left, and the gaping wound in his heart cried out that the pain of rejection was not something he ever wanted to feel again.

All these feelings had come together into a firm resolve as he rested against the ancient stones of the keep. Never again would he allow another to enter his heart. He would keep the world at an arm's distance. Like the images he captured on his camera, he would view the lives that others lived, but he would keep his life separate.

The picture of the castle reminded him of the resolution he'd made on that rainy day two years ago. He'd been true to his vow ever since, and he didn't see it ever changing.

The only reason he'd returned to Utah now was that most of his college friends were still in the area. Even though he had no interest in dating and the memories of his time here with Laura continued to mock him, he would enjoy spending time with his friends.

If he'd been in his new apartment already, he would have just invited Will over for dinner there. Instead, he now had to have dinner at Will's sister's house. He grimaced at the thought. He had nothing against Will's sister. He just hoped Will wasn't trying to set him up. He knew that Ammon had no interest in meeting potential dating candidates.

The only woman he had any interest in was the one that he'd never met in person. Ammon paused a moment to open his wallet and remove a worn photograph from one of the pockets. She, the woman in the photo, was the most captivating person he'd ever seen. He would never meet her, but he thought about her almost every day.

With a sigh, he slipped the photo back into his wallet and grabbed his keys. He needed to leave now to make the drive over to Will's. They were carpooling to dinner, and he didn't want to be the reason they were late.

He was happy to be seeing Will again at least. He liked Kate, and he had no doubt he could make it through one meal with Will's sister. He could be engaging when he wanted to be, and, after all, how remarkable could one dinner be?

*****

Will pulled up in front of Lily's house, and he and Kate turned to look at Ammon in the backseat. He was looking up at the house with a modicum of interest in the flowers Lily had growing in the front yard. They saw his gaze follow the branches of the tall oak tree near the driveway before turning toward the beech tree on the other side of the lawn. Will and Kate shared a worry-filled glance before getting out of the car. Ammon was not the same since his breakup with Laura, and they still weren't quite sure how to navigate his new somber disposition.

He hadn't mentioned his ex-fiancée when he'd met them at their house, but they could tell she still affected him. They had hoped that some time away from Utah with his work would have brought a genuine smile back to his face, but it was still forced and didn't reach his eyes. Ammon followed them to the front door, and they could see his public persona drop into place. They knew he possessed the ability to make others feel comfortable and at ease even if he just wanted to be left alone to brood.

Will shook his head slightly at Kate as they reached the door. She was opening her mouth, and he knew he had to forestall her repeated question of Ammon's willingness to be here. The sound died on her lips, and she shrugged her shoulders at him, willing to follow his lead.

Will felt a slight stirring of guilt at bringing Ammon here but crushed it swiftly before he could change his mind. Truth be told, he hadn't forgotten about dinner with Lily at all. He had a feeling that she, out of anyone they knew, would have the right personality to bring Ammon to life again, if only for the evening. Lily loved knowing about everything and everyone, and he knew she would appreciate hearing about Ammon's work. Perhaps that would be enough to coax him out of his despondency.

He thought it best not to let Lily know about his plan, however. It was better for her to think he was forgetful than to give her cause to think that he was setting her up with Ammon. Neither of them would appreciate it, and he was rather fond of the idea of his limbs remaining intact.

*****

After a quick knock, Will opened the door a crack. "It's open!" a voice from the kitchen called, and Ammon was momentarily caught off guard at the pleasant alto tone. He had never met Will's sister before and, come to think of it, never seen a picture of her either.

Will had kept some family photos around when they were roommates, but he'd never paid them too much attention. He had been distracted by other things and other people. He stopped his thoughts right there before he went too much further into those memories. Thinking of Laura would only make it harder for him to be social tonight, and he didn't want to disappoint Will.

He heard the sounds of conversation beginning and quickly turned his attention back to the present. Will and Kate had walked around the corner and into the kitchen to be with Lily. As he paused in the living room, he heard pieces of the conversation.

"How was the drive? Not too much traffic, I hope," he heard Lily say.

"Nah, not too bad. Since they finished most of the construction on the freeway, it's a lot faster now. At least until they start the next project," Will joked.

Road construction was an ongoing point of amusement and frustration to the residents of Utah county; just as soon as one road project finished, another began. It made a great game, trying to figure out different routes to places so as not to be caught up in the construction-related traffic jams.

"And how are you, Princess?" Lily said. Ammon could hear the grin in her voice at the nickname, and he raised an eyebrow at the expression. He would have to ask Kate where that moniker came from.

"Oh no, not you too," he heard Kate groan in exasperation, but the rest of her comments were lost to him as he suddenly caught sight of Lily's pictures on the wall. The pictures, with a few exceptions for family photos and some religious scenes, showcased the locations Lily must have traveled throughout the world: monuments in Washington DC, sculptures from the Louvre, a nice shot of the Eiffel Tower, the Parliament building and Big Ben from the shore of the Thames, and various scenes of nature from different spots around the globe.

The one that held his attention, however, rested above the piano and featured a castle sitting on a craggy cliffside, standing sentinel amidst a turbulent sea. The picture was magnificent, but it was the castle itself that set his heart racing. He knew that castle, and the sudden sight of it threw him off guard.

He couldn't believe that it was just a coincidence. Did Will know about his trips there? He couldn't recall talking about them with anyone, but perhaps in an unguarded moment he had mentioned them. Had Will brought him here because his sister had traveled to Scotland as well? Perhaps he thought Ammon would want to talk about visiting the castle with someone who had also been there. He found he wasn't angry at that idea, but he also had no interest in discussing something so close to his heart with a stranger. He would have to make sure the conversation stayed on safer topics.

Ammon turned away from the picture, racking his brain for a way to avoid talking about the castle. However, because the piano was on the far side of the living room, he hadn't realized that Will, Kate, and Lily had left the kitchen and were now standing behind him. He opened his mouth to make an off-handed remark that would distract them away from his true thoughts, but he froze as he caught sight of Lily.

The wavy strawberry-blond hair was pulled up in a messy bun, and her head was cocked slightly to the right as she regarded him. Her lips held the promise of a beautiful smile, though they were currently half raised in amusement at his continued perusal of her person. He suddenly realized his camera hadn't done justice to her eyes; it hadn't captured the depth of feeling and perception that he now saw there.

Ammon felt as though he'd seen a ghost. He'd thought about the girl in the photo steadily over the last eighteen months. Now here she stood, and he had absolutely no idea what to say. Will must have seen his shock because he slowly started to smile and raise his eyebrows.

Oh, not good, Ammon thought. He definitely knew he had never told Will about the girl from the castle or the fact that her picture rested even now in the wallet in his back pocket. A wallet that suddenly felt like it was burning a hole in his shorts. He had to cover his surprise, and fast, before Will started becoming even more curious.

"Will, you didn't tell me what a world traveler your sister is," Ammon began, reaching desperately for a way to shift their focus off of him. "Lily, isn't it? I've really enjoyed looking at your pictures."

Wow. That was smooth, Ammon thought to himself with a groan. Had he really just given her the exact opening to talk about the castle that he'd hoped to avoid? He saw her opening her mouth and jumped to speak again before she could ask him a question.

"Dinner smells excellent. Anything I can do to help?" he asked swiftly. He saw her quirk one eyebrow at the redirection, but she allowed him his privacy and started turning back toward the kitchen.

"Everything's ready to go. Come on back to the dining room. I hope you like spice," she said over her shoulder with a smile.

*****

Dinner consisted of spicy chicken enchiladas along with a salad and some fruit. After a blessing on the food, everyone dug in. Ammon noted that Will served himself three large enchiladas without hesitation. Kate noticed too and said with a smile, "Are you sure you can eat that much?"

"Heck yeah! These are Lily's enchiladas. They're amazing! Plus, I'm starving. It was a long day at work, and I skipped lunch,"

Will stated as he finished piling his plate with salad on top of the enchiladas.

Will worked as a civil engineer and his latest project included designing structures for oil refineries. Ammon knew that Will was always running against a deadline since his boss constantly dumped more projects on him than one person could handle. Will had a good sense of humor about it, though, and always managed to finish on time.

"What about you, Ammon?" Lily asked. "What do you do for work?"

That question, though innocent, could get a little too close to some truths Ammon hoped to hide. He took his first bite of enchilada, aiming to stall as he worked out his answer, but seconds later his eyes started watering, and he had to smother a cough as he reached for his drink.

"Oh, did I mention that I made this batch extra spicy?" Lily said with a grin. "I guess Will didn't warn you that we have a bet going about who can stand the most heat."

"Just give up, Lily," Will garbled through a mouthful of food. "You know I'm going to win. And you should have warned Ammon to take his enchiladas from the other side of the pan."

"Don't talk with your mouth full, it's disgusting," Lily retorted. "And I forgot to mention it to him because I was too interested in watching your reaction. You could at least act like it's hot. I added lots of extra peppers on that side.

"Sorry about not warning you," Lily continued, now addressing Ammon. "I'm so used to Kate knowing to take hers from the other side of the pan that it slipped my mind to mention it to you. You can put yours back and get a milder one if you want."

Ammon shook his head. "I like heat. I was just surprised at first. I'll keep it, as long as I can put a little more sour cream on it," he finished with a smile. Lily smiled back, and he felt like he had passed some sort of test that he didn't know he was taking. He liked the feeling of approval her smile endowed. Though he hoped that next time he ate with her, she wouldn't be trying to destroy his taste buds like she was currently doing with Will.

Whoa, did he just think about a *next time*? That thought completely opposed everything he had promised himself. No relationships. Not ever again. But then, he did have her picture in his wallet.

"A photographer? Well, that's exciting!" Ammon tuned back into the conversation just in time to hear Lily's reaction to his profession. Will must have answered her earlier question while he was lost in thought.

"Where have you gone?" Lily asked earnestly, turning toward him. "I love seeing new places. Do you have a favorite?"

"Just about everywhere," he answered honestly in response to her first question. He spent the next hour recounting his travels to all parts of the world and telling her about photographing people from Africa to Asia to North and South America, capturing images of the ruins of ancient civilizations, and spending hours trekking through archaeological sites to record evidence of man's footprints on earth. He never answered her question about his favorite place as he carefully left out his explorations of Dunnottar Castle.

Ammon watched Lily as he talked. She appeared enthralled with his descriptions of the places he had been and the people he had met. He could sense her envy of all that he had seen, and this impacted him. He wanted to know what part of his adventures she found the most compelling.

"I must admit I'm jealous," Lily declared as she stood and started clearing away dishes. "I would love to be able to see the things you've seen."

She'd given him the perfect opening, and he wasn't going to waste it. "What intrigues you the most?" he asked while helping her gather the food to put away. He wasn't sure why he was holding his breath waiting for her answer, but he wanted her to love it for the same reasons he did. He didn't want to think about why that was so important to him.

"It's the people—the history behind every object, whether big or small, tells their story. You can stand there and just feel what it must have been like to be them, to have lived as they lived," Lily answered. She put the dishes in the sink and turned to him fully. "I saw you looking at my picture above the piano. It's Dunnottar Castle in Scotland. My mother's ancestors were from a town not too far from there. Though they never lived in the castle, I went there and could picture what their lives were like living in a feudal system and depending on a castle for protection in times of war.

"And there's just something about castles," she continued as she turned back to the sink and started water to soak the pans. "They're majestic, and yet the reasons they were built primarily have to do with war. It's quite the contradiction. But standing within one, touching those stones that people have touched for hundreds of years, you can't help but feel connected."

"Now you've done it," Will teased. "You got Lil on her soapbox about history and ancient things."

"Just because you don't have an appreciation for the past doesn't mean no one else does," Lily retorted as she flung water in Will's direction.

Will and Lily kept bantering about their different views of history, but Ammon barely heard them. He was trying his best not to stare at Lily, but he couldn't help himself. She'd explained perfectly why he was so passionate about his photography. He wanted to capture the past and bring it alive exactly as she'd described.

He couldn't stop himself from thinking about Lily; he wanted a reason to be around her and get to know her. Something about her enticed him in, even though he was trying to fight it. The real Lily was just as alluring as her picture in his wallet.

4
chapter

Lily quickly finished the dishes and went to pull out a game while Will and Kate wiped the table in preparation for playing. She turned down the hall and flipped on the light as she went. She saw movement out of the corner of her eye and started a little when she realized Ammon had followed her. He was so quiet she hadn't even known he was there.

Ammon must have noticed her slight jerk. "Sorry for startling you. I hope you don't mind that I came with you. I'm curious about the games you have," he explained.

"Oh, it's fine," Lily said as her heart rate came back to almost normal. She continued down the hall and told herself that her heart was still beating a little fast from the scare, not from the fact that Will had failed to mention that Ammon was gorgeous, intelligent, and completely out of her league.

As she reached for the closet door handle, she took another glance at Ammon out of the corner of her eye. He was a little taller than her 5'10", perhaps 6'1" or so. He was obviously no weakling as Lily could see his arm muscles straining his sleeves slightly, though she doubted he was a gym rat. More likely, his muscles came from hefting equipment and trekking into his job sites. The rest of his body was slender, with the well-defined calves of a runner displayed by the cargo shorts he wore.

His hair was a brownish blond, and Lily could tell there was some curl in it, though it was almost too short to be noticeable. His most arresting feature in Lily's mind, however, were his eyes. They were the purest, lightest blue she had ever seen, like the color of a glacier. She thought she could stare into their depths and see his soul. She could tell he was hiding some of his thoughts tonight, but she imagined that, if she knew him well, she could read them all in those very expressive eyes.

"You have a lot of puzzles," Ammon stated. With a slight jolt of longing, she turned her attention back to her task at the game closet.

Lily glanced at him to see if he seemed put off by the puzzles, but his open expression caused her to say, "I love puzzles. I think they're relaxing, though I know they drive most people crazy."

"I like puzzles too," Ammon said with a smile.

"Well, come do one with me anytime," Lily responded lightly. She reached past the puzzles and other games and selected the one that she and Will always played when he came over.

"*Lord of the Rings* Risk?" Ammon asked with a grin. "I never would have pegged you for being a closet nerd."

"Nothing closet about it," Lily said as she pulled the door shut again. "It's a family tradition. We're all complete nerds. I'm surprised Will didn't force you to watch all the extended versions of the movies with him when you were roommates. I thought it was the rite of passage for all his new friends."

"He didn't have to," Ammon replied as they walked back down the hall. "I own them myself. Besides, nerds make the best friends."

He was too good to be true, Lily thought to herself a few minutes later as she set up the game. She glanced up and saw Kate observing her with a little too much wisdom in her eyes. Lily blushed slightly and looked down. The one downside in their friendship was that Lily never could hide anything from Kate, but she hoped Kate wouldn't mention her obvious interest in Ammon to Will. He would make way too big a deal out of it. Besides, guys like Ammon weren't interested in pursuing her, so it would never amount to anything anyway.

"Earth to Lily," she heard Will say. She looked up again to see Will smirking at her and holding up his hands. "Are you planning on picking a side sometime this century?" he teased as he rocked the two pieces he held back and forth in the air.

"You know I'm always Elves," Lily said defensively as she grabbed at the piece in Will's right hand.

"True enough," Will replied calmly, "but I'm still waiting for the day that you acknowledge that the Orcs have the better chance to win with the lands they get at the start."

"That may be true, but the Elves are the good guys. I'm always going to choose them," Lily answered with finality.

"You just like them because you think Legolas was hot in the movie," Will sniggered.

"Well, that too."

"What about you, Ammon?" Will asked. "Elves or Orcs?"

"I think I'll go with Elves," Ammon responded with a glance at Lily. "That way I can harass you about it when we win."

"Dream on," Will scoffed. "I'm feeling lucky tonight." He rubbed his hands together with glee and began placing his players on the board.

Ammon turned to Kate in confusion. "Don't you play?" he asked.

"Oh, no," she replied immediately. "Someone has to remain neutral and remind these two that this is just a game. They forget sometimes."

Lily and Will both briefly stuck out their tongues at her.

"I'm surrounded by children," Kate sighed.

*****

The game lasted a little over an hour, and this time the Elves conquered the board. Ammon watched in amusement as Lily, all maturity forgotten, danced a victory dance around Will. He could tell by the joy in their eyes that neither of them really cared about who won; they just enjoyed being in each other's company.

Kate nudged him and said, "Nice rolling. It's about time Lily won. Will's been needling her about it for weeks."

"Just glad the dice liked me tonight," Ammon responded with a smile. After watching Kate playing umpire throughout the game, he realized that her easygoing nature and quick wit really were a perfect match for Will's more focused but fun personality. He experienced a moment of envy that Will had found someone so suited to him.

"Don't get too used to winning Ammon," Will teased, breaking into his reverie. "If you pair up with Lily more often, you'll soon see that she's usually on the losing team."

"Oh, for the love." Lily smiled exasperatedly. "You can never lose with grace, can you?"

"Nope. Goes against my principles," replied Will seriously.

"All right, you two," Kate intervened, "we don't want to scare Ammon off from ever playing games with us again. Plus, it's getting late and someone has to get up early tomorrow," she ended with a pointed look at Will.

"You're right, hon. Lil, the honor of putting away the game belongs to the victor, so I'll just leave this mess for you. I guess there's an upside to losing after all," Will joked.

"A price well worth paying," Lily responded easily as she reached over and hugged Will goodbye. She gave a hug to Kate, and then Lily was standing right in front of him. Before he knew it, she moved closer and gave him a short embrace as well. She pulled back quickly, almost like she was embarrassed for invading his personal space like that. She turned abruptly back to Kate to confirm a girl's date for the next week, but he still caught the hint of a blush on her cheeks. He smiled as he walked toward the door.

*****

Ammon glanced back at the house as he grabbed the door handle to Will's car. As he situated himself in the backseat, he saw Lily wave quickly from the front window before closing the blinds for the night. His mind was so inundated with thoughts that he hoped Will didn't expect too much conversation from him on the way home. He didn't think he could manage much more than one- or two-word responses right now.

Lily was even more amazing in person than he could have imagined. Though he had looked at her picture often over the past eighteen months, he now found the woman in the photograph not only stunning but exactly the kind of person with whom he could easily fall in love, and that right there was the problem. When her picture was only a private Mona Lisa, someone to keep him company on lonely days without a real commitment, he felt safe. Now his world was rocked by the idea of actually letting someone in again. Memories of Laura and the thought of going through that kind of trauma again caused a brief shiver of fear to run through him before he quickly regained control.

"Cold?" Will asked from the front seat as he started the drive back to his house. Although the summer days were warm, nights in the high desert could still get a little chilly.

"Just for a moment. I'm fine now," Ammon responded, grateful for an excuse that would enable him to hide his true feelings.

"I'm glad you came tonight," Will grinned. "It was great having you along, and I think Lily appreciated the extra company. It's good for her to be able to talk to people like you that have traveled a lot. She loves hearing about that kind of stuff. Thanks for indulging her."

"My pleasure," Ammon stated sincerely. "She was fun to talk to as well, and I always love hanging out with you too, Will. Especially now that I get to taunt you with my win for the next little while. Beats staying at the hotel and cooking for myself any day."

Will laughed as Ammon smiled in the back seat. He could see that Ammon's slumped and worn-down posture was replaced by a slightly more relaxed and contented aura. He congratulated himself that his brilliant idea of bringing Ammon to Lily's had worked out. Lily was good medicine and always managed to brighten everyone's day.

Yup, I'm a genius, Will admitted to himself as he grinned.

5
chapter

A few weeks later, Lily mindlessly changed into her scrubs at work. The hospital mandated that anyone who might be in the operating room had to wear hospital laundered scrubs, and the OR was always a possible destination when working in labor and delivery. Lily didn't mind, however, because then she wasn't the one responsible for cleaning up the stains she acquired on her uniform each shift.

"Lily!" she heard a voice exclaim. Lily turned to see her good friend, Trixie, come bounding into the locker room.

"Trix! I missed your face! How was your vacation?" Lily asked excitedly as she gave Trixie a brief hug.

Beatrice James, or Trixie as she vastly preferred, grinned widely. "Absolutely amazing! Definitely put it down on your list of places to go. In fact, I'd totally go back with you anytime. I've never seen anything like it."

Lily groaned a little in envy. Trixie had gone on an Alaskan cruise, which included stops in several ports along the peninsula. Starting in Seattle and ending in Vancouver gave her the added highlight of touring those two cities as well. Lily had wished to go too, but it was a last-minute trip and she couldn't rearrange her schedule in time.

"I still can't believe you just left me here alone for two whole weeks!" Lily sighed. "The nights were torture without you here to keep me awake. Plus, I'll bet you managed to find Prince Charming on the cruise, and now you're going to leave me here while you run away to your own little kingdom."

"Oh, stop it." Trixie laughed as she started changing into her scrubs. "You know I did no such thing. I hung out with my cousin the whole time, and I was too busy eating the amazing food and climbing the rock wall on the back of the ship to notice guys anyway."

Lily just smiled to herself as she bent down to slip on her socks and shoes. Trixie might not have noticed the guys on the ship, but she wagered they had noticed her. Trixie was stunning with her green eyes, dark brown hair, athletic figure, and quick smile. Lily couldn't understand how in the world Trix was still single. She finally decided it was because Trixie was clueless when it came to realizing that men fell all over themselves around her. She was the nicest person and treated everyone so well that she probably never even thought about the effect she had on people.

Lily stood up just as Trixie finished pulling on her scrubs. As she reached for her shoes, Trixie asked, "Is it busy tonight? I didn't look at the board before I walked in here."

"It's not too bad, just five labors and a couple of triage patients."

"Here's hoping it stays nice," Trixie said as she crossed her fingers. "I want time to catch up with you. Pick a patient near me so we can chat!"

"Can do," Lily saluted. "I'll go find some close together while you finish dressing."

"Just not a primip!" Trixie shouted as the door to the locker room closed.

Lily grinned. It would serve her right after leaving her for the last two weeks if Trixie ended up with a first-time mom, or primip in labor nurse lingo, as a patient. First-timers were generally the sweetest patients with whom to experience birth. It was a thrill to see the patient and her husband as parents for the first time. On the flip side, however, first babies usually took a couple of hours or more of just pushing before they delivered, and spending that much time coaching someone could be exhausting. Plus, if she signed Trixie up for that she likely wouldn't be seeing her a lot tonight.

"I guess payback will have to wait for another night," Lily muttered as she walked toward the charge nurse's station. At her hospital, the nurses were allowed to choose their own initial assignments. As the shift progressed, the charge nurse would give them more patients as they finished with their originally chosen patients.

It was the role of the charge nurse to make sure everything ran smoothly, patients were cared for correctly, and the floor nurses had the support they needed for the different labor situations that occurred during the shift. *Not an easy job*, Lily thought, grateful that she only performed in the charge nurse role on rare occasions. She found she preferred taking care of patients to taking care of everything else.

She quickly found two assignments next to each other. They had the potential of not being too time-consuming. She wrote down her name and Trixie's, then walked toward her assigned area. Nine hours later, at three in the morning, Lily and Trixie finally sat down together at the nurses' desk. They both heaved a sigh of relief and then, looking at each other, laughed at how the night had unfolded.

Lily had chosen two seemingly easy patients. Hers was a third-time mom, and Trixie's was a lady who had delivered her baby right before they got there. A delivered patient usually just needed an hour or two of recovery time to make sure everything was stable before she transferred to the post-partum ward. Unfortunately, Trixie's patient started hemorrhaging about thirty minutes after they began their shift. It took several medications, a manual removal of some bloody clots, and finally an emergency blood transfusion before the patient's condition stabilized.

Lily always marveled at how complex the labor and delivery process could be. She knew most people thought the mom came in, everything went according to the birth plan, and in a few short hours labor climaxed with the delivery of a perfect, new little life. Often it did go like that, Lily admitted, but then randomly things could go wrong. In a moment, things could change from anticipating a new baby to rushing around trying to save lives.

Trixie's patient didn't have any risk factors for hemorrhaging other than it was her fifth baby, though it was a researched fact that the more children a patient had, the more likely it was that a hemorrhage could occur. Lily rejoiced that the patient at least delivered in the hospital where they could respond to the situation quickly and hopefully avoid any serious side effects. Still, it got the adrenaline going and the heart racing every time there was a serious emergency. Then, once Lily finished helping Trixie with her patient, Lily's own patient was ready to deliver.

Now, both of their patients were finally on the maternity floor now, and they had a moment to relax. Happily, the charge nurse said they didn't have new patients to take at that time, so they were free to relax for a moment.

"Do you think if I get out my food, I'll actually be able to eat it? Or will it cause more patients to walk in?" Lily joked.

"You can try it if you want to," Trixie replied, as she leaned back in her chair and closed her eyes. "I think if I eat, though, it'll put me in a food coma, and I'll fall asleep right here on the desk. My body thinks I'm a normal daytime person again. It's not used to being awake at three anymore."

"My heart cries for you in your suffering," Lily said sarcastically.

Trixie smiled widely but kept her eyes closed. "Tell me something to keep me awake." She yawned.

"I'm boring," Lily lamented. "The only interesting thing in my life is that my brother brought an old roommate over to dinner a few weeks ago. He is gorgeous and absolutely fascinating. But it doesn't matter," she quickly continued as Trixie opened her eyes looking excited. "It's not like he got my number or has any intention of seeing me again. I'm guessing he hasn't thought about me at all. You know about my luck with men."

"I think you underestimate yourself. You are a catch, and any sane man would be lucky to have you," Trixie retorted. She held up a hand as Lily looked to interrupt. "Nope, it's true, and I won't have you telling me otherwise."

"Whatever you say, Trix," Lily said, rolling her eyes.

"Well, I think you should ask your brother for this guy's number and ask him out on a date."

Lily looked at her like she'd grown horns. "Are you serious?" Lily asked incredulously. "There's no way I can do that! First, Will will think I'm crazy, and then he'll make fun of me for the next millennia. Plus, I doubt Ammon even wants to see me again. Especially not on a date."

"Why ever not?" huffed Trixie. "Honestly, you're your own worst enemy, Lil. You have so many amazing pieces that make up you. There's got to be something you guys have in common."

"Well," Lily hedged a bit, "he did seem interested in my traveling. Though he was probably just being polite and asking since he travels tons with his job."

"You're ridiculous," Trixie rolled her eyes. "Fine, if you won't admit he could possibly be interested in you, then I won't push it. But for now," she continued brightly, "let's get superficial. Describe him to me so I can at least picture this guy you think is so attractive."

Lily laughed and happily spent the next several minutes expounding on Ammon's features until another wave of patients walked in and kept them busy for the rest of the night.

6

chapter

Two weeks later Lily hummed to herself as she finished putting up the last of her fall decorations. She wasn't what she termed to be "cutesy" by any stretch of the imagination, but the decorations she did have made her smile.

Her crowning piece of decor was a blown glass pumpkin she'd purchased in Vermont on a girls' trip with Kate. They had watched in awe as the glass blower created magnificent pieces from the multi-colored glass beads in front of him. This was a treasured memory and one that she relived every time she displayed the pumpkin in the fall.

The trip was also memorable for some of the most delicious apple cider doughnuts she had ever had, and thinking about them now caused an instant craving for them. Fall baking was another favorite tradition of Lily's once September arrived. She rubbed her hands together in anticipation of the cinnamon smell that she intended to have emanating from her kitchen in short order.

As she reached for her recipe book, her phone rang. She looked down to see a number she didn't recognize. Most of the time unidentified calls were just solicitors and she let them go to voicemail, but for some reason she picked it up.

"Hello?" Lily said distractedly as she put the recipe book on the dining table and began flipping pages to find the one with the doughnut recipe.

"Hello, is this Lily?" a melodic voice asked. "This is Ammon, Will's friend. You let me crash your family dinner several weeks ago."

Lily sat down heavily on a nearby chair in surprise. In a feat of impressive proportions, she managed to not drop the phone in shock. "Hi, Ammon. Yes, this is Lily. How are you?" she replied flustered. Why in the world was he calling her? Did he leave something here? Her eyes quickly surveyed the room, though she knew nothing there was out of place.

"I'm great. I just got back in town from my last assignment. I'll be in the country for a few days, and I was wondering," he hesitated, "if I could take you up on that offer to do a puzzle?"

For a moment Lily sat dumbfounded trying to figure out what he was talking about. Then it dawned on her that she had told him he could come over and do a puzzle with her. She just never thought he would actually do it. "That sounds fun," Lily finally blurted out. "I don't work again for the next few nights, so I'm free whenever."

She knew admitting that went against all the hard-to-get lessons her girlfriends had tried to teach her, but she had never liked playing those games anyway. Hopefully she didn't sound desperate to Ammon though.

"Great! Is tonight too soon?" Ammon asked.

"Not at all," Lily responded, though surprised that he wanted to see her so quickly. "In fact, I was just about to make some apple cider doughnuts, so there should be a few here to snack on while we work."

"Oh, those sound good. I haven't had those in years. I'm glad I picked today to call."

"I'm glad I'll have someone to share them with so I don't eat them all myself."

"A win-win situation then," Ammon laughed. "Does six work for you? I'm pretty sure I remember how to get to your house."

"That'll be perfect, and if you get lost, just give me a call," Lily answered brightly.

"Will do. I look forward to seeing you tonight, Lily."

"You too."

As she ended the call and placed the phone on the table, Lily realized that she was feeling lightheaded and reminded herself to breathe. So the object of her affections desired to spend an evening with her. That was still no reason to suppose they would be anything more than friends, she told herself. But inside, despite her best efforts, a flame of hope sprang into existence, and Lily found herself grinning widely as she started making the doughnuts.

*****

Ammon pulled up to Lily's house and turned off the car. It turned out his new apartment was so close that he didn't need to drive over, but he didn't want to explain arriving on foot to Lily. He found himself hesitating to get out and, when he looked down at his hands, he realized they were a little shaky. "I'm nervous about seeing a girl," Ammon muttered in astonishment.

Normally, he controlled his emotions so well that most people couldn't tell what he was thinking unless he expressed his opinions out loud. Tonight, his thoughts were so turbulent he wasn't sure what he might blurt out. He'd gotten her number from Will a few weeks before on the pretense of sending her a message to thank her for including him in their dinner. He'd told himself at the time that he wasn't going to use it to come see her. Eventually, however, he's curiosity about Lily got the best of him, and he wanted to see if his attraction to her would fade in closer proximity. He'd become steadily more anxious about seeing her again until he'd finally broken down today and called. Now that he was here, he hoped he could keep his scattered thoughts in check around her.

Taking a deep breath, Ammon got out of the car and began the short walk down the sidewalk to the front door. He noticed with new eyes the changing leaves on the towering oak tree next to the driveway, the flower bed under the big front window, and the bold red door sitting at the top of the three steps that led up to the porch. It was all neat and tidy, and the house stood out in its own way compared to the others on the street. "Just like Lily, understated perfection," Ammon quietly remarked to himself.

He knocked before he lost his courage and waited as he heard Lily's steps approaching. Out of the corner of his eye, he caught a flash of her figure through the big window on his left and then she was there, opening the door. She was stunning, though Ammon knew it wasn't her casual, albeit tasteful, clothes that made her so. It was the light in her eyes, he realized as he stared at her. Their brightness made everything else about her seem extraordinary.

"Come on in," he heard Lily say cheerfully, and he somehow made his frozen muscles move him off the porch and into the house.

"Thanks for letting me come on such short notice," Ammon remarked as he stepped inside. "My job makes advanced planning difficult to say the least."

"I'm glad it worked out," Lily responded. "Though I'll admit it took me by surprise that you called. I honestly didn't think you would actually take me up on my puzzle offer. I thought you were just being polite when you said you liked them."

"Well, as much as I do like puzzles, I find I enjoy your company even more," Ammon found himself declaring. What was he saying? It was the truth to be sure, but he wasn't here to confess how much he liked her. He had come to spend an evening with the girl from the picture, convinced that she couldn't possibly be as entrancing as she seemed. Now he was almost admitting to her that he had feelings for her. He would have to be more careful in what he said so as not to lead her on.

Lily blushed, looking embarrassed, and turned away slightly at his words. "Thanks. The puzzle's in the dining room. I took the liberty of flipping the pieces over already. I hope you don't mind."

She started walking across the living room, and Ammon was struck by the thought that perhaps she wasn't used to getting attention from men. He was both saddened and heartened by the notion. She merited notice, but at the same time he was selfishly glad she hadn't been scooped up by some other guy before he had this chance to spend time with her. Part of him wished that he could dote on her like she deserved, but that would mean opening his own heart again. He was definitely not ready for that.

"Do you like doing the edges or picking a specific part of the picture to start with?" Lily asked as she sat down at the table.

"Whichever," Ammon replied honestly, taking his own seat next to Lily. "Do you have a preference?" He looked over at the puzzle and noticed that it was a Thomas Kinkade scene featuring houses on a river in the twilight. Quintessential Kinkade; peaceful, relaxing, and full of light.

"I like to start with the windows on this puzzle," she answered, grabbing a few pieces. "There's something about how light they are that makes me happy."

He smiled as Lily then reached for a plate on the counter next to her and handed him the platter of doughnuts before he had even begun to reach for the edge pieces.

"Fortification for the fight ahead." Lily laughed as her eyes twinkled.

He knew she had no idea about the inward fight he was having not to reach for her hand instead of the puzzle pieces. Before his thoughts could betray him, he filled his own hands with a doughnut and a puzzle piece and turned his attention away from Lily and her tempting smile.

*****

Lily smiled as she unconsciously hummed to herself. She had turned on some light classical music before Ammon arrived to keep herself from thinking too much. As a classically trained pianist, she could listen to instrumental compositions for hours. She loved the feelings the music evoked. Currently, Beethoven's seventh symphony, second movement was playing, which happened to be her absolute favorite piece. She glanced up momentarily and noticed Ammon looking at her with a small smile on his face.

They had chatted about his latest projects, her work shifts, and a few of their adventures from the last month. Lily discovered that Ammon's photography work stemmed from a love of history and the outdoors. He had majored in history in college, with a minor in photography. He said he got his minor because he loved being out in nature and wanted to be able to better capture the beautiful vistas he saw while hiking in the mountains. It just so happened that his job combined the three things he loved the most. Lily felt a little jealous listening to him. She loved her job, but she'd majored in nursing because it was the practical choice. If she'd really followed her dreams, she'd be digging up archaeological sites in the Middle East.

Eventually, the conversation had waned and they lapsed into silence. However, the quiet wasn't uncomfortable at all. Lily felt relieved that his personality was such that he enjoyed time in his own thoughts as much as speaking aloud. She found that many people were uneasy if she wasn't constantly talking to them, but those relationships wore her out quickly. She preferred quality over quantity when it came to conversation.

"What?" Lily asked Ammon, slightly shocked that he had been watching her without her realizing it.

"Did you know that you were humming along?" Ammon grinned.

"Was I?" Lily's eyes widened in chagrin. "Sorry about that. It's an old habit, and this is my favorite song."

"Oh, don't apologize," Ammon said quickly. "I like the sound of your voice. Tell me about this song. I'm not familiar with it."

Lily smiled and, after telling him the title, began describing the piece and why she enjoyed it so much. She could tell by the way Ammon leaned toward her as she spoke that he cared about what she thought, and she found herself amazed that he found her ramblings interesting. Most guys tended to tune her out pretty quickly when she started in on something about which she was truly passionate. They seemed disconcerted by either her increased rate of speaking or the myriad of details she added when discussing different topics.

"I can tell you really love music," Ammon commented as Lily finished her explanation.

"I do," Lily concurred. "There's something about good music that speaks to the soul. No matter what you're feeling, there's a song that expresses your emotions perfectly. Sometimes it's easier for me to play the music than to try and voice my thoughts out loud."

"I have to agree with you. Music expresses my thoughts much more clearly than I can. Whenever I try and say what I'm thinking, especially if it has to do with feelings, the words get all jumbled and confused. I can't really convey what I feel," Ammon admitted.

"Too true," Lily said, nodding. "Still, Will always tells me that I speak my true feelings too quickly. Apparently, it's off-putting. But what's the point of not saying how you really feel about things? I'm not going to *not* be myself just to make someone more comfortable. Besides, if I did that, then I'd end up being around people who don't appreciate the real me. I think I would rather be alone than lonely in a crowd."

*****

Ammon's mouth hung open as he was suddenly flooded with the feeling that Lily was exactly who he wanted in his life. She was not only beautiful outside, but she possessed the purest soul he had ever encountered. There was no deceit in her, and he wanted to be with her so badly it was like a physical blow.

"I can't date you," Ammon blurted out suddenly.

Lily looked up at him in astonishment. Her eyebrows raised, and she stuttered slightly saying, "That's not what I meant when I was talking about feelings."

"I know," Ammon interrupted. *Smooth.* What was he supposed to say now? He had felt such a strong need to tell her how he was feeling because he knew if he allowed himself to be around her without some barriers in place then they would both end up damaged.

"It's just," Ammon took a deep breath and continued, "I like you, Lily. The more I'm around you, the more I want to keep being around you. But before I give you the wrong idea about my intentions, I just needed to warn you that I have promised myself to never be involved in a romantic relationship again."

"Okay," Lily said slowly. "Why would you do that, if you don't mind my asking?"

Ammon wasn't sure how much he wanted to tell her, but the confusion and hurt on her face prompted him to be truthful. "A couple of years ago, I was engaged to a girl. Laura was her name." Ammon paused. It hurt just thinking about it, but he knew he needed to continue. "I thought we were perfect together. I thought she was everything I wanted, but two months before the wedding, she started acting strangely. It took a couple of weeks to get her to admit to me that she had actually started seeing someone else and wanted to break up with me."

"Oh, Ammon," Lily cried out softly as she covered her mouth with her hand.

"It broke my heart, though I tried to act like it didn't in front of her. I didn't want her to see how badly she'd hurt me," Ammon related distantly. He relived the horrible night again as he talked about the incident. The anger, grief, and sheer shock of it lingered even now. "The worst part was having to call everyone and explain that there wasn't going to be a wedding. I hate being the center of attention, and this was the worst kind of attention to receive," Ammon continued after a moment. "Everyone was kind of course, but I swore to myself I would never put myself in a position to feel that way again."

Ammon looked at Lily as he finished his story. He wanted her to understand why he had to maintain a distance, to see why he couldn't ever be more than a friend.

"I'm so sorry that happened to you," Lily uttered softly as she briefly placed a comforting hand on his forearm. Though she removed it quickly, the spot where she touched burned, and Ammon regretted once again his decision to remain aloof.

"I'm glad you at least decided to spend an evening with me," Lily responded lightly, trying to lift the mood after his confession. Though he knew he had hurt her feelings, he was grateful she chose to respond positively.

"We can still be friends, if that's okay," Ammon said hesitantly. He loved her company but didn't want to torture her with his presence if it was too hard on her.

"I'd like that." Lily smiled slightly. "Now if you don't mind, friend, you're hogging my pieces." With that she reached across him and gathered up several of the pieces near the edge of the table on his side. Ammon laughed and helped her find what she needed before continuing on with the puzzle himself. He silently breathed a prayer of thanks that Lily allowed him to stay.

I can be a good friend to her, he promised himself, *but she deserves someone so much better than me.*

7

chapter

"You're kidding!" Trixie exclaimed a few nights later as Lily finished telling her about the puzzle incident, as she'd taken to calling it.

"Nope. I wish I were. I really like him, Trix, but what can I do to change how he feels? Whoever Laura is, she did a number on him. I can't make him suddenly decide he's ready to date again if he isn't," Lily moaned.

Taking a quick glance at her fetal monitors, Lily sighed. She had been doing a lot of that since Monday's puzzle night. It was now Saturday evening, and she finally had the chance to talk to Trixie. Lily tended to work every Wednesday, Thursday, and Saturday night, but Trixie mixed it up a little more, so it was always a treat when their schedules coincided.

"The worst part," Lily continued, "is that he wants to be my friend. Not that that's bad," she added quickly, "but if he really means it, I'll be around him knowing that no matter what I do, I'll never have a chance."

Trixie raised an eyebrow but remained silent. Lily dropped her head onto the desk and groaned, "I'm a fool."

"Yes, you are," Trixie replied immediately. Lily looked up at her and glared.

"You said it, not me!" Trixie laughed, but then she sobered. "Seriously though, Lil, I know you. You're so giving that you'll be this guy's friend even if it kills you. But I'm worried about you. Are you really okay with this? You need to think about how you feel too."

Lily paused as she thought about what to say to Trixie. She had thought through her conversation with Ammon more times than she

41

could count, and still she didn't know what to make of it. Oh, she knew he had meant what he said, but why even establish a friendship with a person you liked if you never intended on dating them? But every time Lily prayed about what to do, she felt good about continuing to see Ammon. It made absolutely no sense. How could she make Trixie understand what she didn't understand herself?

"I think this is something I need to do," Lily said slowly. "I don't know why, but it feels right to have Ammon in my life. Even if it's just as a friend."

Trixie looked doubtful but said, "Well, I still think you're crazy. I'll support you and be here to pick up the pieces if this guy breaks your heart, but I'll also egg his house if he does."

Lily laughed. Trixie would never really do it, but it felt good knowing she was looking out for her. "I'll make sure to get his address then," Lily announced with a grin.

"You don't know where he lives yet?" Trixie asked.

"No. He left again on Wednesday for a work assignment before I ever had a chance to go over to his place. He said he would call when he gets back. I guess we'll see if he actually does," Lily remarked.

Just then Lily's patient called out, and she got up from the desk to head into the patient's room. "You better keep me updated!" Trixie called as Lily headed down the hall. Lily flashed a thumbs-up in Trixie's direction as she walked away.

*****

The next Friday night, Lily sat in front of her closet bemoaning the fact that she cared nothing for fashion. "It's all well and good not to care until suddenly you want to look your best for a guy taking you out on a *not-a-date*," Lily muttered nervously.

Ammon had called yesterday and asked if she would like to go to the local planetarium to see the constellation presentation. During their puzzle night, they had discovered that they both had an interest in astronomy, though Lily admitted that Ammon's knowledge in that subject far surpassed her own. In fact, she was coming to find that he possessed a surprising store of information about a plethora of topics.

Since she found intelligent men to be the most appealing, his brain was now as attractive to her as his well-formed physique.

Lily pursed her lips as she pulled out yet another blouse and then discarded it just as quickly. "I need Kate," Lily admitted, but for once in her life, Lily hadn't been telling Kate everything. She wasn't ready for Will to know that she and Ammon were friends, and as soon as she told Kate she knew he would find out. That would lead to him asking questions she couldn't answer. So she purposefully stayed mum about her activities with Ammon.

Heaving a sigh, Lily picked out one of the previously set aside shirts and pulled it firmly over her head. "It doesn't really matter what you look like anyway," she grumbled to herself. "He only sees you as a friend, so you might as well wear something comfortable."

Ammon had hinted on the phone that they might be outside at some point tonight, though he kept the reason a secret. With that in mind, Lily finished dressing in layers that would work for both a warmer inside and a cooler outside. Just as she finished gathering her things, the doorbell rang. Despite herself, Lily found her heart rate increasing as she hurried to the door.

"Foolish." She grinned to herself as she made one last inventory of her accessories and then let herself out onto the porch.

*****

Ammon thought he had braced himself for another encounter with Lily, but then she opened the door and all his barricades went tumbling down. She glowed with excitement, and he wished it was all for him and not for the planetarium.

"Ready?" Ammon asked needlessly as he tried to firm up his resolve once again.

"Absolutely!" Lily exclaimed. "I love the planetarium. I can't wait for the show tonight." She brushed her hand across his arm for a moment and then practically jumped off the porch as she made her way to the car. "Coming, slowpoke?" she called as she drew near the car.

Ammon laughed and hurried to catch up to her so that he could open her door. She smiled in thanks as she sat inside. They kept up a lively conversation as they drove to the planetarium and walked inside. Within a few minutes of their arrival, the lights dimmed as the host welcomed them and gave an overview of the program for the evening. Ammon noticed Lily giving the ceiling her rapt attention as the room fully darkened and the artificial, though beautiful, constellations started playing across its domed canopy.

The presenter began telling legends that revolved around the Cassiopeia and Andromeda formations that were currently visible in the night sky. As the tale grew to include Perseus and the love story he shared with Cassiopeia, Ammon felt himself wanting to hold Lily's hand. He knew he shouldn't, so instead he leaned over and asked softly, "How would you feel about gazing at the real thing when we're done in here?"

He noticed with satisfaction that her smile widened as she looked at him. "I'd love it. Let's get out of the city and go somewhere we can really see them."

"Done," he replied with a wink. He sat back in his seat again, happy that he had prolonged their time together. He turned his own eyes back toward the presentation overhead, though he didn't stop himself from occasionally glancing at Lily through the rest of the program.

*****

Ammon kept his promise to find a secluded place away from the light pollution of the city in order to see the stars more clearly. They followed a main road for several miles west and then drove down some old farming roads until a small mountain range stood between them and the bright city lights.

"Beautiful," Lily breathed as she emerged from the car. She glanced up and turned in a circle as she took in the majesty of the heavens. "The Milky Way is so clear out here. And there's our friends Cassiopeia and Perseus," she added, pointing.

"Yes, they are," Ammon responded with a slight sadness in his voice as he came up beside her. "They're so close together yet destined to never cross the space that separates them."

Lily glanced up at him with a small crease in her brow, but before she could respond, Ammon looked down at her and smiled. "How would you feel about stretching out on a blanket across the hood of my car so we can lean back on the windshield and really enjoy the view?" he asked.

"Do you have one?" Lily looked back at the car in surprise.

"As it so happens, I do," Ammon replied as he opened his trunk. He gallantly handed Lily a blanket as he reached in for a second one. "One for beneath us and one for on top. I'll give scouting the credit for helping me always be prepared," he added with a cheesy grin.

Lily giggled as she spread her blanket and then climbed onto the hood. Ammon bounded up beside her and spread his blanket across their legs. Although the night wasn't freezing cold, the crispy fall air certainly had a bite this late at night, and the blanket felt good as it captured their warmth. Lily leaned back against the window and, after a slight hesitation, Ammon followed.

"Which constellation is your favorite?" Ammon inquired.

"Orion," Lily answered promptly. "In fact, if you promise not to make fun of me, I'll let you in on a little secret."

The tone of conspiracy in her voice made Ammon smile. "I promise," he vowed.

"He's my confidant. I tell Orion all my thoughts, feelings, and frustrations. He's a rather good listener," Lily continued seriously. "He's always up when I am too; night shifts throw me off, so I often find myself wide awake at four in the morning. Instead of lying in bed, I go for a run, and while I'm out, I look up at Orion and tell him all my woes." She looked over at Ammon and winked as she finished, and he chuckled at her playfulness.

"You know," he intoned, "Orion is my favorite too. Perhaps one of these days, he'll whisper some of your secrets to me, and then I'll know all your thoughts."

Lily laughed. "Well, if you really want to know, I'd recommend skipping the middleman and just asking me directly. Otherwise, we'll end up playing a celestial version of telephone, and you know that game never quite gets things right."

"I'll keep that in mind," he replied, mock seriously. He then spent the next several minutes pointing out different celestial features, some of which Lily never even knew existed, like luminous blue variables. During his discourse, Ammon placed his arm on Lily's bent leg and rested his hand on her knee. She stiffened for a moment and then relaxed at the warmth of his hand. She rarely allowed men to get this close to her, and this incident marked the first time she had actually relished a friendly touch from a guy.

Don't make a big deal out of it. He probably doesn't even realize it's there, she chanted as she tried to reason with herself, but she couldn't deny how good it felt to have him close. She snuggled a little closer to him until their shoulders were touching. He smelled so good, and the heat radiating off his body was intoxicating. She normally regretted the fact that her body temperature ran low, but her perpetual coolness now gave her an excuse to nestle in closer to him without feeling too guilty about it. "Trixie's going to kill me if I ever tell her about this," Lily muttered softly to herself.

"Sorry, what was that?" Ammon inquired. He had gradually lapsed into silence a few minutes earlier and seemed almost startled to hear her speak.

"Oh, nothing," Lily hurriedly replied. "I was just wondering, what's your favorite time of year for viewing constellations?"

They entered into an enthusiastic debate about the relative merits of summer versus winter constellations. It carried them through the next hour until they finally decided they should make the drive back before it got too late. Lily immediately regretted losing Ammon's touch but knew it was best for her own sanity if she tried to forget it lest she lose her heart to a man that didn't want it.

8
chapter

Several weeks later, Lily knew she was in deep trouble. She had spent time with Ammon every day that he was in town. Even when she worked back-to-back night shifts, she would often emerge from her wake-up routine to find him on the porch waiting to see her. On her days off, she often walked over to his apartment. Together they would walk to a nearby park and play Frisbee, climb a tree, or just amble around the neighborhood. They could walk for miles sharing stories and laughing or quietly enjoying the beauty of the changing season around them.

Lily teased Ammon good-naturedly when he finally confessed to living only half a mile away from her. He told her he had moved in after their first meeting, though he had already signed the contract beforehand and he said he didn't want her to think he was a creeper. She laughed and told him it was the first time a guy had moved to be closer to her, and she would take it as a compliment. He pretended to wipe sweat off his forehead in relief, and from that day on she had an open invitation to come over.

Though he hadn't physically touched her again as he had the night they viewed the stars together, he had entwined himself so thoroughly around her heart that she knew she was falling in love with him. "Oh, what an idiot I am," Lily sighed aloud. She bemoaned the fates that led Ammon into her life when he was so solidly bent against being more than friends.

She thought once again about Ammon as she gathered her belongings for work. He had been out of town for the last few days but would return tonight. Though she wouldn't see him until tomorrow, she grew excited at the idea of spending time with him again. "I'm a glutton for punishment," she said out loud. "But I just can't seem to help myself."

*****

She was hoping for a busy night at work to distract herself from her thoughts of Ammon, but in all her imaginings she couldn't have predicted what would transpire during this particular shift.

Since the labor and delivery floor at her hospital was a high-risk unit and saw hundreds of deliveries a month, Lily helped to deliver lots of babies. But there were also patients on the floor for various reasons besides active labor, and tonight Lily had chosen a newly admitted one that was there for PPROM at twenty-one weeks.

Lily knew people often thought of her job only in terms of holding babies after a successful delivery. Whether through ignorance or a willful desire not to think of what could go wrong, most people didn't know how often complications could and did arise. So many things threaten the lives of both the mother and the baby. Working in a high-risk hospital probably skewed her view somewhat, Lily admitted to herself, but she possessed a great appreciation for the miracle that life truly was and how fragile it could be.

PPROM, literally "preterm premature rupture of membranes," is a dreaded complication when it happens before the fetus is viable at twenty-four weeks. Without the membrane, or bag of water, to protect the baby, infection is a huge and common complication. Preterm labor and subsequent delivery are the other likely scenarios resulting from a lack of amniotic fluid, but other than administering a few medications, there isn't much to be done for PPROM patients besides waiting to see what the mother's body would do.

According to the previous nurse, Lily's patient was stable; she had no contractions, appropriate movement from the fetus inside, and no infections brewing that could be detected. These were all positive signs. The amount of leaking amniotic fluid had slowed through the day, and everyone was optimistic that they could keep

the baby inside at least until viability at twenty-four weeks and hopefully beyond.

Lily greeted her patient, Amy, after getting report on her situation from Lisa, the off-going nurse. Amy was alone, she had been
told, though Lisa didn't know if there was a significant other involved
or not. It had been a busy day shift, which didn't leave much opportunity for Lisa to spend time digging into the personal lives of her
patients if they didn't volunteer the information upfront.

Lily, with only Amy to care for at the moment, decided to try
and solve some of the mystery surrounding Amy's situation. She felt
like she should, if for no other reason than to know who to call if
something should go wrong in the night. After half an hour of idle
chitchat, Amy finally revealed that the father of her baby was somewhat involved but not emotionally tied to her.

"It was more than a one-night stand," Amy confessed hesitantly.
"At least, on my part. But what I didn't know at the time was that he
was also seeing someone else. After I got pregnant, he told me that he
would help support the baby but didn't want to stay with me."

Lily held her temper in check as she took Amy's hand. It
wouldn't help to start raging about the type of low-life men that
would, in essence, abandon their own children. She would save that
soap box for a conversation later with Trixie. It was, unfortunately, a
situation they both saw far too often.

"Amy, you are a beautiful and wonderful woman. I have no
doubt that you deserve so much more than you've been given. I hope
at least tonight I can ease some of your worries and be a support for
you. What can I do for you?" Lily asked.

She spent much of the night talking with Amy about her fears,
the realistic expectations of her condition, and the resources they
could tap to help her financially. Lily gently asked if there were any
other family members she could call to be with her, but Amy just
shook her head and teared up, so Lily left it alone.

They visited until two in the morning, when Lily walked away
for a moment to help in another room. As she stepped out into the
hall again thirty minutes later, she could see Amy's call light on. She
frowned slightly as she walked toward the room. She had thought

Amy was tucked in for the night and had hoped Amy would be able to get some sleep. Lily knocked softly and opened the door.

She knew immediately that something was wrong. Amy, who hadn't complained of pain all night, was suddenly flushed, sweating, and breathing hard. Lily knew what this meant and struggled to hold back her tears. She rushed to Amy's bedside while using her phone to call the resident doctor to come and evaluate her. When she received no response, she left a message about what was happening and then called the charge nurse. She glanced at Amy while doing so and knew that she didn't have much time left.

"I'm sorry, Lily," the charge nurse answered distractedly as her call finally went through. "We had an emergency come in, and the on-call doctor and resident are both back here in the OR." Lily could hear the noisy commotion of a turbulent OR and knew that she would receive no help from that direction.

As she hung up the phone, Lily took a deep breath and turned to Amy. Amy's eyes were closed in concentration as yet another contraction wracked her body. As the pain subsided, Amy looked up with tear-filled eyes and whispered, "The baby is coming, isn't she?"

Lily's heart constricted at that moment. Before confirming Amy's fear, she replied, "I won't know unless I check your cervix. The doctors are busy right now. Would you mind if I examined you?"

Amy closed her eyes and nodded for Lily to proceed. It took only a moment for Lily to use a speculum to visualize a pair of small feet making their way through the birth canal, followed closely by the rest of the body. Lily closed her eyes in sorrow, again choking down her own tears, then looked up at Amy.

She knew Amy understood without her saying anything, for a silent sob shook her body just as another contraction commenced. Once it passed, Amy looked up and simply uttered, "How long?"

"Not long," Lily answered softly. "Would you like me to call anyone for you?"

"I already tried before you got in the room," Amy confessed. "No one answered."

Lily's heart, already torn, broke a little more at the news. No one should be alone in moments like these, and yet Amy was. "I won't leave you," Lily affirmed quietly. She quickly set up a delivery table while trying to support Amy through her contractions. Sooner than she anticipated, it was time. She took a moment to send a quick call to Trixie for some help and then prepared to deliver Amy's baby.

As Lily tenderly guided Amy through the delivery, she heard a soft pair of feet walk through the room toward the infant warmer. She glanced up momentarily and saw Trixie standing there, waiting to assist if needed. She smiled sorrowfully in thanks for the help then turned her attention back to Amy.

With only a small effort, the baby girl delivered. Lily gently lifted the precious bundle onto the blanket she had placed on Amy's chest. She wrapped the blanket around the baby as Amy reached her arms around her quiet daughter.

Though she was born with a heartbeat, the sweet baby girl never tried to breathe. Within thirty minutes Trixie, who stayed in the room to monitor the baby, listened intently for a moment through her stethoscope, then shook her head as she failed to hear the heartbeat any longer.

Amy's tears slid quietly down her face in a waterfall of sorrow as Lily continued sitting by her side for long moments after the baby passed. Eventually, the resident walked softly into the room, and Lily rose to tell her in a quiet tone all that had transpired. The resident shook her head sadly and then moved to talk with Amy before examining her.

Lily remained in Amy's room for the next few hours before transferring her to post-partum to finish recovering. In all that time, no one ever came in to see Amy.

As soon as she completed Amy's transfer and its associated charting, Lily made her way into an empty room. She slumped against a wall and slid down until she was sitting on the floor. She curled her arms around her legs, put her head on her knees, and cried.

9
chapter

Her crying session didn't last as long as she wished. Though her shift was nearing its end, a few more walk-in patients needed to be examined. Lily dried her tears and mechanically went to work, trying her hardest to give smiles she wasn't feeling to patients who had no knowledge of what she had just been a part of and who were only excited about their own upcoming deliveries.

That morning as she changed back into her street clothes, Trixie came up and put her arms around her. Normally, neither one of them was much for hugs, but this time Lily knew she needed it and willingly accepted her friend's show of comfort.

"What are you going to do to cope?" Trixie quietly asked as she stepped back. She knew not to ask if Lily was okay; no one with a heart was ever okay right after witnessing a tragedy such as they had.

"I'll find someone to talk to today. I promise," Lily replied.

With a nod, Trixie walked over to her locker as Lily tiredly began the trek out to her car. Mentally she reviewed her list of support people. Her parents, especially her mother, would always answer her calls and talk whenever she needed it. But they, for the first time in forever, were actually on vacation, and she didn't want to cast a pall over their trip. Will and Kate were probably busy getting ready for the day since it was six thirty in the morning and they both had to be at work by eight o'clock. Her younger brother, Jack, was in Europe on a study abroad, and she didn't really want to talk to him about it anyway.

Sighing, Lily knew she was making excuses for her family members. Any one of her family would be happy to take her call and let her sort through her feelings, but the person she most wanted to talk to was Ammon. Reaching her car, she climbed inside and dialed Ammon's number before she could talk herself out of it. He generally woke early, but even so she crossed her fingers that she wasn't disturbing him.

"Lily? Are you okay?" Ammon sounded concerned as he answered on the second ring.

"Not really," Lily replied, trying to fight back a fresh wave of tears. "Work was difficult tonight, and I could really use someone to talk to."

"Come over," Ammon responded immediately. "I'm just reading in the living room. I'll watch for you to pull up."

"Thanks," Lily whispered and hung up the phone. She concentrated on seeing through the tears in her eyes enough to drive, though her spirit already lifted with the thought of having Ammon there to help her sort through her emotions.

*****

Ammon opened the door before she could even knock and quietly led her inside to the kitchen table. He pulled out a chair for her and then sat down next to her with a look of concern on his face. Lily took a deep breath and then slowly unfolded the events of the night to Ammon. She could see his hurt and anger at Amy's situation and his sorrow as she explained the delivery and the outcome. Her tears were mostly gone, though a few slipped out again as she described the beautiful baby girl.

Seeing her tears, Ammon grabbed her hand and held it softly as Lily took a few deep breaths to calm herself. Just feeling his warm touch and seeing his concern helped her feel safe and cared for. Lily found the tightness in her chest relaxing and turning from sorrow to peace.

"Thank you for being willing to listen to me," Lily said softly. "When bad things happen at work, it's always tragic. But seeing Amy going through it all alone just made it that much harder."

"I'm just glad I'm here," Ammon replied. "I was reading St. John when you called, and I think the verse I stopped on applies. Would you like to hear it?"

"I would," Lily responded with a slight smile.

"'Peace I leave with you, my peace I give unto you: not as the world giveth, give I unto you. Let not your heart be troubled, neither let it be afraid,'" Ammon read quietly.

"Thank you," Lily whispered, a few fresh tears shining in her eyes.

Ammon didn't respond aloud but instead stood up, pulled Lily up next to him, and enfolded her in his arms. Lily allowed her eyes to close as she clung to him like a life preserver. Her head rested against his upper chest and shoulder, and she could faintly hear his steady heartbeat. It was a soothing sound. Gradually, the warmth of his body began to lull her to sleep, and she reluctantly pulled away before she actually passed out on him.

With promises to return that evening, Lily made her way back out to her car and home. Ammon's calm acceptance of her emotions and his willingness to listen to her made her glad once again that he was part of her life. She felt considerably lighter after her time with him and hoped that the peace she felt would stay with her as she slept.

10
chapter

Holding Lily's hand and hugging her earlier that morning had breached the last resistance of his crumbling personal barrier, and Ammon found himself looking for reasons to touch Lily now that she had slept and returned to his apartment.

Lily had the night off, and they had planned a pumpkin carving contest for that evening. With Halloween only a few days away, Ammon figured the pumpkins might even survive without being smashed by trespassers before the actual holiday.

In preparation for their contest, Ammon had purchased two large pumpkins and collected an array of knives and other implements to assist in their carving. In order to make it fair, they agreed to freehand their designs instead of using paper drawings on the pumpkins.

Ammon rubbed his hands together in excitement, and Lily laughed at his exuberance. "Are you sure you can handle this?" Ammon teased her, playfully pulling one of her braided pigtails.

Lily looked affronted and, placing her hands on her hips, retorted, "I have two brothers. I've learned a thing or two about carving these beasts. Plus, I think I might be a better artist than you, so watch your back." She took the sting out of her words with a wink and a gentle nudge, and together they gathered their supplies and began the work of pulling the innards out of the pumpkins.

An hour later, Ammon looked up from his pumpkin and declared his masterpiece completed. Lily, absorbed in her own work, looked up and then began laughing so hard she had to sit down on the floor. "What?" Ammon asked, grinning. Lily glanced up but didn't answer as the chuckles continued escaping her lips.

Looking down at his pumpkin, Ammon let out a laugh as well. He had next to no artistic talent, so his pumpkin featured the generic triangle eyes, nose, and mouth that any grade schooler could carve. Around the back side, however, he'd cut out the words "student loans" and surrounded them with images of pain and suffering.

"You have to admit, they're pretty scary," Ammon joked. "Happily, I worked as a carpenter through college, so I never had any. But many of my friends did, and they're still paying those suckers back."

"I'll hand it to you," Lily replied, wiping the tears of laughter from her eyes. "You managed to create a very scary pumpkin. We might have to give you the win for creativity alone."

Ammon grabbed Lily's hand and pulled her to her feet. Turning her around toward her own pumpkin, he lightly placed his hands on her hips and looked over her shoulder. She shivered slightly, and when he looked at her, he saw her trying to hide a smile. Smiling himself, he looked down at her pumpkin. Lily definitely had more creativity than he did, he admitted. She had managed to carve the *Star Wars* emblem into her pumpkin and then shaved the skin in places to create two lightsabers in battle.

"Wow, Lil!" he exclaimed. "That's amazing. I can't believe you did that freehand."

Lily blushed and looked pleased. "I've been wanting to try this for a while, but I wasn't sure it would work out. I guess it came out pretty well."

"Absolutely. I think we should declare you the winner," Ammon added seriously.

Lily turned around to face him, and Ammon reluctantly moved his hands off her hips. "Co-winners?" Lily offered with a grin, her hand outstretched.

"Co-winners," Ammon confirmed, grasping her hand and giving it a firm shake.

They spent some time cleaning up the pumpkin innards and separating out the seeds. Ammon placed them in a plastic container and handed it to Lily. "I'm leaving to go out of town again tomorrow, and I don't know that I'll be able to bake them up before I go," he said, responding to her questioning look. "In fact, maybe you should take my pumpkin over to your place so you can light them both up on Halloween since I won't be here to do it."

"Better idea," Lily responded with a grin. "You come home with me, bring your pumpkin and those seeds, and we bake them up tonight and watch a movie. I'm going to be up forever anyway, and I give you full permission to fall asleep during the movie if you get tired."

"Good to know." Ammon winked. "But I think I can handle it if it's not some chick flick."

Lily raised an eyebrow and said, "I've got the movie *Valkyrie* at home. It's about a doomed German resistance plan to destroy Hitler. It's about as far away from a chick flick as you can get. I've been meaning to watch it for days. Would that work?"

"Bring it on." Ammon smiled.

11
chapter

After they finished baking the pumpkin seeds, Ammon and Lily walked with their snacks into the addition where Lily kept her washer and dryer, wood burning stove, and the television. The eclectic room highlighted the interesting layout found throughout the house. Built originally in the 1940s, different owners through the years had continued to add updates, rooms, and new fixtures in a seemingly haphazard manner.

Lily loved it. The whole house only contained 1260 square feet, but it boasted three bedrooms, a bathroom, a decent-sized living room, a combination kitchen-and-dining room, and this gem of a back room. She laughed at the person who had thought the washer and dryer should occupy the same space as the wood burning stove but just shrugged at the idiosyncrasy and went with it.

"Hey, Ammon," Lily called, turning excitedly toward her wood pile. "Think it's cold enough for a fire tonight?"

"Definitely. Want me to help you get it set up and going?"

"You're the boy scout," Lily answered with a wink.

With a laugh, Ammon set about starting the blaze while Lily turned on the movie. In no time, they both finished their labors and fell back onto the oversized bean bag chair in front of the TV. Lily noticed that Ammon sat a little closer to her tonight. Granted, even a large bean bag chair tends to roll its occupants toward the middle and touching is basically inevitable, but Ammon usually sat clear on the other side of the bag. Tonight, they were already shoulder-to-shoulder. *Interesting*.

Trying not to make too much of it, Lily settled in beside him, and they both became absorbed in the movie. Being history buffs, they each looked for the little details in the film that added to its authenticity. Pretty soon, they made a game of seeing who could find the most historically accurate element in each scene.

Three-fourths of the way into the movie, Ammon sat forward and gave her a high-five when she noticed a particularly small but meaningful detail on one of the automobiles. As he sat back again, however, his left arm slid firmly behind Lily's back, and he gently pulled her into his left shoulder and rested his head on hers.

Shocked but happy, Lily snuggled in closer. She decided that being right where she was, basking in the glow of a warm fire, and listening to Ammon describe another movie detail he just observed, was the most romantic moment she'd ever had. She didn't know what he meant by his closeness tonight, but she decided to just enjoy the moment for as long as it lasted.

As the credits rolled a short time later, Lily closed her eyes and tried to absorb the feeling of being there next to Ammon. She knew that as soon as the credits were over, he would get up and go back home for the night. It was already midnight, and he generally went to bed by eleven. She leaned in a little closer and took a deep breath of the pleasant smell she associated with him.

"Are you sleeping, Lil?" she heard him ask softly.

Feeling a little guilty for her desire to keep him there longer, she promptly opened her eyes and found him leaning forward slightly and staring down at her. Her words caught in her throat as she tried to decipher the emotions in his gaze. She saw desire there but also caution and a hint of sorrow. She froze momentarily, not knowing what to say. She desperately wanted to ask him what he was thinking about, but she wasn't sure she really wanted to hear it.

"I was just making myself comfortable," she eventually answered, going for lighthearted banter in an effort to still the sudden trembling in her limbs and the butterflies that danced in her stomach. A random thought came to her mind then that butterflies were far too sedate to be performing the acrobatics she currently felt. Perhaps the expression should run more along the lines of cows running a stampede through her abdomen.

"Hmm, yes, it is rather comfortable right here," Ammon responded while easing back down on the bean bag and pulling Lily in a little tighter. "Maybe I'll stay a little longer. Tell me why you enjoy learning about WWII so much."

Lily, delighted to have him there with her longer, launched into a long explanation of why she found the events of that time fascinating. She could hear herself adding more details than were really necessary but couldn't stop the flood of thoughts cascading through her mouth. She knew she should reign herself in, but she didn't want him to stop holding her and figured that when she finished speaking, he would leave.

Eventually, she found herself running out of things to say. Remarkably, Ammon sat calmly through her entire monologue; too calmly in fact. Looking up at him again, she noticed for the first time his closed eyes and deep breathing. *Well, that's just great*, she thought. *I've put him to sleep!*

Just as she began chastising herself for talking too much, Ammon spoke, "Lil, I just love listening to you talk, and I think I'm too comfortable right now to want to move. Will you talk to me about something else? I just want to hear the sound of your voice."

Startled but pleased, Lily racked her brain for something else to say. She began describing the piano pieces currently on her dossier to learn. Soon, Lily noticed Ammon's breathing slow and his head resting heavily on top of her own. Not minding the extra weight, Lily snuggled in closer and ceased to speak. She felt selfish for not waking him up and sending him home, but she enjoyed the chance to cuddle in close and look at him without being caught.

He's so wonderful, she thought with a sigh. *I have no idea what he sees in me. Perhaps he feels like I'm safe. I probably only imagined seeing any desire for me in his eyes. I've never had anyone want me before, so this is most likely a noncommittal cuddle session.*

But even as these negative thoughts bounced through her head, Lily tightened her arms around Ammon and determined to enjoy the moment. Her eyes grew heavy as she memorized his face. Soon they closed, and Lily passed into a peaceful sleep.

*****

Sometime later, Ammon woke and looked down at Lily's sleeping form snuggled in close to him. The light of the fading fire cast a soft glow on her features, and he smiled at the sight. He knew it had to be late judging by how far the fire had burned down. He sighed but didn't release his grip on her.

How selfish I am, he berated himself silently. *She likes you, unless you imagined that flash of desire in her eyes that mirrored your own. If you really want to do what's best for her, you would leave right now.*

But he didn't have the willpower to do it. He cared for Lily. He smiled when he heard her voice and delighted in her witty comebacks. She was beautiful to him, for her inner radiance shone in her face and lit the room with her glow whenever she was near.

He wanted right then to break his vow; he knew he could easily convince himself to do that. Perhaps things would be different with Lily. After all, she was not Laura, and she would never put him through the grief that Laura had. If he really admitted it to himself, he already cared for Lily more than he had for Laura, for in Lily he found an equal.

Ammon wrestled with his thoughts all night. Every time Lily stirred or sighed in her sleep, he looked down and imagined holding her for the rest of his life. It felt right; he felt whole with her. But then he would allow his memories of his past heartache to once more engulf his mind. He grew melancholy thinking about it, and he continued to be torn at the thought of allowing anyone in his heart again.

His thoughts went back and forth all night until the horizon began to lighten with the coming of the new day. Lily must have somehow sensed the gradually brightening sky, because her eyes slowly opened and she softly bit her lower lip as if trying to remember where she was.

Seeing that simple gesture finally overcame his reserves. He had noticed it weeks ago while watching her as she worked on the puzzle. When she concentrated, she would slowly pull her bottom lip in and gently tug on it with her teeth. It was an unconscious motion, but he adored it and all his excuses to stay away from her died away while observing it now.

Before he could stop himself, he brought his head down to Lily's and gently pressed his lips to hers. He felt her small gasp of surprise change into eager acquiescence as he held her softly to him. Her hand, resting on his chest, slowly moved up to his neck as he prolonged the kiss. He kissed her tenderly once more and then leaned back to see her reaction.

Lily's eyes slowly opened again and, as he watched, her lips drew back into a radiant smile. She reached up and stroked his cheek, and Ammon had never felt so wanted.

"I hoped you'd do that," Lily admitted shyly.

"I've wanted to for a long time," Ammon confessed.

Her eyes twinkled with pleasure, and he felt elated to have been the source of her joy. As he leaned in for another kiss, Ammon knew he had changed their relationship forever. He only hoped he hadn't made a huge mistake.

12

chapter

Two weeks had passed and still Lily couldn't stop grinning. Ever since kissing Ammon, she felt like she walked around on cloud nine. Nothing could bring her down, not even the crazy shift she currently found herself enmeshed in. It seemed the entire world wanted to have a baby tonight, Lily thought as she exited her patient's room. Though, with Valentine's Day nine months ago, their busyness made sense.

Trixie walked quickly past and gave Lily a wave as she entered her patient's room. Lily smiled back and went to type up some papers for the triage patient she was discharging. They hadn't been able to talk much tonight as wave after wave of laboring mothers inundated the unit from the moment they had arrived that evening.

Lily admitted to herself that she was afraid of telling Trixie about the latest development with Ammon. She knew Trixie would worry about her feelings being hurt, but Lily wouldn't back away now. She still didn't understand why Ammon would pick her, but she was so happy he had.

Thinking of Ammon made her surreptitiously reach for her phone. She hated to pull it out at work lest a patient's family see it and think she was being neglectful, but Ammon's current shoot took him to Israel and the time difference made night shifts their prime communication hours.

Opening his most recent text, Lily saw he had sent her a picture of the sun rising over the Dome of the Rock in Jerusalem. The photograph glowed with rays of sunlight, and the surrounding vistas looked pristine so early in the morning. Ammon sent a message along with the picture that read, "As gorgeous as this view is, my favorite sunrise is still the one I saw through your window."

"I'm sorry, what is he talking about?" Trixie's voice suddenly spoke out behind her, and Lily nearly jumped from her chair in surprise.

"Trixie! You almost gave me a heart attack!"

"You're in the right place for it if that's the case, but I need you to turn around and explain to me why Ammon saw a sunrise at your house. And don't try and tell me you went out for an early morning jog together, because I'll see right through that one."

Lily sheepishly turned around in her chair with a small grin at Trixie. One look at the arched eyebrow on Trixie's forehead, coupled with her crossed arms and someone-is-about-to-receive-bodily-harm posture, encouraged Lily to quickly try to explain.

"It's not what you're thinking Trixie," Lily hurried to say. "We were watching a movie and talking, and then we both just fell asleep. It's all completely innocent, I promise."

"Hmm. If it's all so innocent, why would it be his favorite sunrise? Don't tell me a poor night's rest on your lumpy bean bag chair brought forth his captivation with that particular dawning. Something happened, and you are going to own up to it right now," Trixie said firmly.

Lily gulped, took a deep breath, and said, "It could also be because we fell asleep cuddling, and when I woke up, he kissed me." She winced and waited for Trixie's reaction. She was not disappointed.

"Lily Manning, have you lost your mind! I thought this was Mr. Never-more-to-be-in-a-relationship. How in the world did you move from hanging out as friends to kissing without discussing that minor hurdle?" Trixie exclaimed. "Lily, I want you to be happy, but are you sure he's not just using you?"

The thought hurt, but Lily knew Trixie only mentioned it out of concern. Truthfully, Lily still didn't know what Ammon thought about their future together. Try as she might, the niggling seed of doubt that he would still walk away couldn't be denied. She thought she knew him well enough to know that he wouldn't hurt her on purpose, but he could easily still hurt her without meaning to.

Lily shook her head to banish her negative thoughts and replied, "He's not using me, Trix. I know you're worried about me, but really, I'm happy. I think the world of Ammon. In fact." She let her voice trail off, not sure she should give substance to the rest of her thought.

"Oh, Lily." Trixie sighed as she sat down. "You're in love with him, aren't you?"

"Maybe a little," Lily admitted timidly. "Is that so bad?"

"No," Trixie acknowledged with a half-smile. "I just overreact when I think people are moving too fast. Forgive me for not having more faith in both of you. I suppose any of our pasts can easily over-shadow the future if we let them."

Lily gave Trixie a look of surprise. It sounded as if Trixie had some ghosts in her closet that Lily knew nothing about. Before she could follow that line of questioning, Trixie stood up, reached out a hand to pat Lily's shoulder, and said, "You're worth having someone love you. If he proves himself worthy of you, no one will be happier for you than me."

Lily watched Trixie walk away back toward her patient's room in wonderment. What in her past caused her to react like she did? Lily's innate curiosity awoke to this new mystery, but she knew Trixie would only share her story if she wanted it known.

Knowing she would have to wait for another opportunity to ask, Lily allowed herself another moment to answer Ammon's text, then got back to her feet to continue on with her assignments. As she walked toward the printer containing the discharge information for her patient, she allowed her smile to return. Ammon will come home tomorrow, and she couldn't wait to see him.

13
chapter

Ammon dropped his suitcase on the floor and collapsed on his bed, grateful to be home. Though he had loved Israel, the political climate there always made his assignments a little harder to accomplish. This time, for the moment at least, the various factions in the Holy Land weren't actively fighting, and Ammon's project had granted him access to various areas around Jerusalem. His photographs there included several scenes of the Old Jewish Quarter and the Wailing Wall, along with vistas of the Al-Aqsa Mosque and the entirety of the Old City of Jerusalem.

A side trip to Bethlehem had also added some panoramas of the believed birth site of Jesus. He wasn't sure of the angle of the piece being published by the magazine, but as Easter was only five months away, he felt confident his photos, along with a historical account of the Holy Land from biblical times, would be featured.

The scenes he saw had been awe inspiring, and he felt grateful for the measure of peace he had gained there. Still, he had spent much of the trip fighting an inner battle about his relationship with Lily.

He couldn't deny that he had enjoyed having someone to talk to every day, even if the messages weren't very long or detailed. Just knowing she was there, wanting to hear from him, made him happy. Plus, he missed her presence and her smile. He looked forward to seeing her again after he slept off some of his jet lag.

However, doubts about the wisdom of entering into another serious relationship continued to assail him. What if he was too broken to be good enough for her? He didn't want to disappoint her with his own shortcomings. Further, his emotional dependence on her scared him. He never meant to be vulnerable to anyone again.

"Ugh," Ammon moaned, placing his hands over his face. It was an impossible quandary. He knew he couldn't have it both ways. He couldn't date Lily without opening himself up to her; she deserved better than that.

Too tired to run through his arguments again, Ammon set his alarm to wake him up in three hours. By then, Lily would be up as well after sleeping off her night shift. Perhaps just seeing her again would help put some of his fears to rest. He rolled over and closed his eyes, trying to shut off his thoughts but having little success.

*****

He contacted Lily after finally giving up on the nap, and soon he heard her knocking on his door and then letting herself in. He had told her some time ago to just barge right in, but he thought it was cute that she always insisted on knocking first. She said she didn't want to catch him streaking through the halls.

Ammon walked out of his bedroom and into the living room where Lily stood taking off her shoes. She straightened, and Ammon noticed that she looked a little unsure of herself. The same small lip-biting gesture came back, and her quiet hello told him she didn't know quite how to act around him now.

Her hesitancy caused him to want to reassure her that he still embraced the change in their relationship. Despite his own doubts, he walked confidently to her, wrapped his arms around her, and leaned in for a kiss. The electricity between them surprised him with the immediate heat it conjured, and he reluctantly pulled back and wrapped her up in a hug before he got too carried away.

Happily, Lily seemed content with his wordless reassurance, and he felt her relax in his arms as her head rested against his shoulder. "I missed you," she said simply a few minutes later.

"Likewise," he replied huskily.

"It was so hard," she continued, "without anyone for me to beat in ping-pong. Honestly, I almost didn't make it."

Ammon glanced down and saw her smirking up at him. He laughed at her playfulness. His normal Lily was back in full force now that she felt sure of her place again. "You saucy minx," he growled, gently grasping her head in his hands and bringing his face within inches of hers. He saw her breath catch and knew he had the upper hand.

"Are you sure you're the one who always wins in ping-pong?" he asked quietly while placing a feather light kiss on her brow.

"Yes?" Lily answered, her eyes fixed on him.

"You sound doubtful. Perhaps we should go play a round and see who the winner really is," he whispered as he kissed her nose and cheeks in succession.

"I might," Lily croaked and cleared her throat, "I might be willing to do that on one condition."

"And what's your condition?" Ammon breathed, his lips a hairbreadth away from hers.

"Hmm?"

"Distracted, Lily?" His lips were so close to hers that he could feel them as he formed his words.

Instead of answering, Lily closed her eyes and leaned in to kiss him again. This time there was no mistaking the fireworks that erupted between them. As Lily entwined her arms around his neck, Ammon found himself wrapping his arms tightly around her and pulling her fully to him. His thoughts were consumed with Lily: her smell, the feel of her close to him, and the taste of her lips.

He knew he should release her, but she felt so good that his body rebelled at the thought. Finally, in a herculean effort, he schooled his emotions enough to bring their kiss to a close. He placed his forehead against hers and was gratified to hear her breathing just as raggedly as he was.

After catching his breath, Ammon opened his eyes and asked, "Your condition, Lily?"

Lily lifted her eyes to his and considered him for a moment. "The loser owes the winner dinner and a shoulder massage," she finally replied.

Ammon smiled in agreement and, reaching down, grabbed Lily's hand to guide her to the ping-pong table. He breathed a sigh of relief that her condition hadn't involved any more kissing, because he didn't know how well he could control himself if they started kissing again tonight.

14

chapter

Wow. Just wow. Lily didn't know how her legs supported her as she followed Ammon back into his game room. She had never been kissed like that before. It somehow melded love, desire, joy, rapture, and belonging all into one earth-shattering embrace.

She still felt dizzy and wondered if it would always feel like that. She imagined that with the right person it would. No wonder people enjoyed it so much! Her previous kisses had been pecks at best and definitely hadn't brought forth the mind-blowing electricity she felt in Ammon's arms.

She wished she could kiss him all night. However, she knew that going further physically right now would only lead to heartache without any guarantee of permanency to their relationship. Lily knew that she attached quickly, and she couldn't just be physical with someone without it being very meaningful to her. So while her condition for playing ping-pong had at first involved a much more intimate agenda, as she looked into Ammon's eyes and felt his control slipping along with her own, she wisely changed the bet to just dinner and a massage.

Maybe she should have left out the massage part as well. Just holding Ammon's hand encouraged the now awakened electricity to continue zipping up her arm to land in every part of her. Hopefully this added awareness could be transferred to fast reflexes during their game, because the rest of her senses seemed strangely disjointed.

Ammon led her through the doorway of the second large bedroom in his apartment. Since he didn't have roommates and the apartment's living room was fairly small, Ammon had transformed this space into a pseudo man cave. The computer he used to edit his pictures stayed in his bedroom out of harm's way, but a slightly more beat-up monitor and console sat on a back table for general use. The ping-pong table stood open in the center of the room since they played together often, but it could be folded up and pushed against the wall if he wanted to pull out the card table and have groups of people over to play games or watch the large flatscreen TV mounted on the far wall. Ammon had told her once that he wasn't a huge fan of TV or crowds, but every now and then he enjoyed having a group of friends over and thought a movie and game night was the easiest way to entertain without having to plan too much.

A couch sat across from the doorway, and Lily gratefully sank into it for a moment while Ammon gathered the paddles and balls. "Ready to eat crow?" he teased as he handed her a paddle and pulled her to her feet.

Feeling slightly steadier, Lily laughed and gently punched his arm as she walked to the opposite side of the table. "If that's what you're making me for dinner when I win, then perhaps I should make you take me out to eat instead."

Ammon laughed and they soon fell into the familiar routine of hitting the ball back and forth to warm up. Once officially started though, the game was intense on both sides. Lily felt like they were each putting all their pent-up emotions into playing and, while the game was still friendly, it was definitely more competitive than usual.

At last Ammon was one point away from winning. However, they played rally score tonight, and Lily was only a couple of points behind. She served a particularly difficult ball to Ammon that he just managed to lunge and reach. It made its way back over the net but put him standing past the far-left corner on his side of the table.

Lily smiled as she hit the ball back, aiming toward the right-handed corner of the table where he would have no hope of reaching before the ball bounced away. She was ready to celebrate her point when, out of the corner of her eye, she saw Ammon's arm swing. Her mouth dropped open as she watched Ammon's paddle, now free of its owner's hand, fly perfectly perpendicular to the ball and actually manage to intersect it at the exact right moment to return it back over the net. It should have been an easy return for Lily, but she froze in surprise. Before she could react, the ball bounced off her side of the table and past her.

"Yes!" Ammon shouted in triumph.

Lily's mouth still hung open, and she turned to see him perform a little celebratory dance, his grin as wide as the Grand Canyon. "How? What? Wait…how did that just happen?" Lily finally stuttered.

"You, my dear, just got schooled, that's what." Ammon laughed.

"But…that's not…you can't—" Lily couldn't quite decide how to protest because that move should never have worked. But somehow it had, and Ammon, currently walking happily her way, was clearly the winner.

"I can, and I did," he said, throwing an arm across her shoulders. His other hand removed the paddle out of her hand and gently set it on the table before he turned and began walking them from the room. "Face it, Lil. I'm just *awesomer* at ping-pong than you."

Lily grimaced at his purposeful poor grammar and poked him in the ribs with her elbow.

"Ow," he complained, though the grin never left his face.

Lily sighed. She knew she was beaten and, with an epic ending like that, she couldn't complain either. "All right," she conceded, moving toward the kitchen. "What do you want me to make you for dinner?"

*****

Ammon watched Lily as she created pumpkin waffles and buttermilk syrup to go along with their breakfast-themed dinner. Every now and again, she looked up at him and smiled, and he felt himself growing more excited about the idea of making their dating relationship official and having the right to call her his.

Lily put Ammon in charge of the bacon and eggs after he insisted on helping her, and they talked as they worked. Their conversation highlighted another reason he liked Lily; she showed genuine interest in his work. They often discussed the historical impacts of the ancient civilizations he preserved in photographs with as much gusto as many people talk about football.

Their discussion continued as they sat down to dinner, though Ammon's thoughts were distracted as he began digging into his waffles. "Dang, Lil, these are amazing." He moaned as he put another bite into his mouth.

"Thanks. There's nothing like pumpkin and cinnamon in the fall." She smiled, happily eating her own portion and then reaching for another piece.

They continued talking and laughing through dinner as Ammon's stories switched from the historical places he photographed to the different kinds of people he had met in the streets of Jerusalem.

"I've always wanted to go there." Lily sighed as she set down her fork at the end of their meal. "But I think my parents would kill me if I went alone, and none of my friends have wanted to go with me."

"I'll take you," Ammon replied without thinking.

Lily's look of surprise made him consider what he said. He really did wish to see the Holy Land again through her eyes. He knew she would have insights about different historical sites that he had never thought of before. "I've got some friends over there right now," he continued quickly. "I'm sure they'd be more than happy to put us up. Then we could travel up and down the country and visit all the places you've always wanted to see."

Lily looked skeptical. "That's kind of a big trip. Are you sure you want to do that? With me, I mean."

Ammon regarded her seriously. Suddenly, all the off-handed comments designed to turn attention away from herself made sense. "Lil," he said gently, taking her hands, "why don't you think I'd want to take you? I like being with you. I think you're an amazing woman. Perhaps no one has ever told you that before. You are unique in the most wonderful way. You're intelligent, kind, beautiful, and giving. Your competitiveness gives me a run for my money playing games, but then you'll listen quietly to me for hours if I just need to talk. It's quite the alluring combination."

He saw her eyes glisten for a moment before she pushed the tears back. "I," she started weakly, then swallowing continued, "I guess I just don't see myself as having much to make me stand out. My family loves me and I have good friends, but guys never seemed to want much to do with me. So I just figured I wasn't enough somehow. At least, not in a relationship. In fact—"

"Yes?" he asked softly after a moment.

"You're the first guy who's ever wanted to actually get to know me," she whispered with her eyes downcast. "No one else ever stuck around. I've had so many people tell me it's because I know too much and that's intimidating. You're the first guy I haven't intimidated, I guess."

Ammon knew she meant that as a compliment to him. He stood up from the table and, pulling her up beside him, wrapped her in a huge hug. "You could never intimidate me, Lily," he promised, chuckling softly but tightening his grip to help her understand that he acknowledged her fears.

"Even if I start blabbering out random facts about the origin of ice-skating or the latest research in stem cell therapy?"

"Even then."

Lily sighed happily and snuggled into his hug. "I'm so lucky I met you."

I'm lucky too, Ammon reflected. His thoughts turned once again to the picture he still carried in his wallet and the remarkable woman he held in his arms.

15

chapter

The holiday season made seeing each other a little more sporadic, but they enjoyed the opportunities they did have together by going snowshoeing, taking long walks, getting into snowball fights, and playing endless rounds of ping-pong and chess. Lily thought she was good at chess until she played Ammon. Though, admittedly, most of the times she lost it was because Ammon distracted her as she tried to think through her next moves.

Ammon also took her out to Indian food for dinner one night to celebrate her birthday since she would be gone on the actual day. Lily loved naan and a vegetable coconut kurma more than anything, so it was already the perfect date to her. Plus, Ammon encouraged her to splurge on a mango lassi, and her taste buds danced for joy as she relished the yogurty drink.

Then, after they finished eating, Ammon handed over the present he brought, and Lily opened it to find a ping-pong paddle inside. She had complained to him lately that the pads on the one she frequently used were wearing out. This new one he got her wasn't an expensive model, but he lacquered the handle for her to add some extra smoothness to the grip. It touched Lily that he would go to the trouble of adding that personal detail. Had she not been in a public restaurant, Lily felt she could have expressed her gratitude with more than the small kiss and hug they shared in the booth.

A couple of days later, Lily went home to Arizona for Thanksgiving. It so happened that this year her birthday and Thanksgiving fell on the same day. So she got up early and ran a

Turkey Trot with her family and then prepared to celebrate her "Happy Thanksbirthday," as she had taken to calling it.

Ammon sent messages throughout the morning, wishing her luck on her run and then encouraging her to replace all her burned calories with extra pieces of pie for him. His work had assigned him to travel back east to photograph the sites of the original Thanksgiving for an online article to be posted by his magazine. Conveniently, his family hailed from upstate New York, so he was spending the actual holiday with them.

She saw Ammon sporadically the next month, as work kept him busy traveling for much of December. Before she knew it, it was Christmas Eve. Lily loved Christmas, and even working through the night couldn't dampen her enthusiasm for the holiday. She bounced around excitedly throughout the evening, socializing and enjoying the decorations hung throughout the unit. She and her fellow nurses, patient free for a miraculous moment, also indulged in platters of Christmas goodies and watched Santa fly around the world on the online Santa Tracker.

She was sad that she wouldn't be seeing Ammon until after the New Year, though. A last-minute schedule change at work allowed him to be home for Christmas this year. She wanted him to know she was thinking about him, however, so as soon as it hit midnight in New York, she sent him a message wishing him a merry Christmas. A moment later she was surprised to hear a text come through with the most cryptic message he'd ever sent.

"Turn around?" she read out loud confused.

She looked up to see her fellow nurses grinning. Dawning comprehension filled her as she quickly pivoted toward the doors. There he stood, holding a potted poinsettia and grinning from ear to ear. With a little squeal of joy, Lily rushed over and wrapped him in a huge hug. After a moment, she remembered where she was and turned around blushing. Some of her coworkers were laughing, and others just smiled. Her charge nurse told her to go use an empty waiting room for a little while; she would call if she needed her to come back to the floor.

Lily led Ammon down the hall, and they sat together in a vacant waiting room. Lily chose the one decorated for the hospital's annual Christmas decorating competition. The area currently featured a cardboard fireplace complete with glowing flames, Christmas lights strung across the walls, and an array of Santas, stockings, and snow-flakes on the windows. A few festive pillows displayed through the room perfected the cozy atmosphere, and Lily found herself feeling blissfully happy as she and Ammon sank together onto one of the couches.

Ammon held her hands and kissed her a few times before sitting back against the cushions with his right arm around her shoulders, his left hand continuing to run up and down her arm producing the most delicious shivers.

"Not that I'm not happy to see you," Lily began, "but how are you here?"

"Well, I spent a few days with my family after my last assign-ment ended," he said, "but I knew you'd be alone for Christmas since your family is out of state. So I decided to surprise you and spend Christmas with you."

Lily grinned as her heart filled with joy at the idea of being with him on her most favorite day of the year. "Do I get you the whole day?"

"As long as you want me."

"I'll always want you," she warned good-naturedly. "Will you come over as soon as I get off in the morning?"

"Don't you want to sleep?"

"Not if you're there waiting for me."

"Then I'll be there. Maybe if you're lucky, I'll even cook some special Christmas cinnamon rolls for you."

Lily raised an eyebrow at that. "You know how to cook cinna-mon rolls?"

"In fact, I do," he replied. "As long as you have a recipe you wouldn't mind me borrowing."

Lily laughed at that and promised she did. She agreed to let him in on her secret cream cheese frosting recipe too since it was the only frosting she really liked on cinnamon rolls.

After another thirty minutes of chatting, patients began trickling onto the unit and the charge nurse called Lily to come back and help. Ammon gave her a short kiss and hug good night and promised again to be at her house when she came home.

Feeling completely happy, Lily floated through the rest of the night. What a perfect Christmas surprise.

16
chapter

True to his word, Ammon's car waited in Lily's driveway as she pulled up that morning. He reversed to give her enough room to get by him and into the carport before pulling in behind her. The sky was clear and, though the sun hadn't yet crested the mountains, a full moon still shone on the new snow that had fallen through the night causing it to glisten merrily. Lily's icicle lights glowed outside, and the lights on her tree peeked through the blinds of her front window. An idyllic Christmas wonderland, he thought, stepping out of his car and meeting Lily at the back door.

She quickly entered into the back room, placed her poinsettia around the corner on the kitchen counter, threw her coat and scarf onto the coat pegs fastened into the wall, and shut the door behind him after he walked inside. He barely had time to remove his own coat before she threw her arms around his neck and pulled him into a lingering kiss. He eagerly returned the embrace, and for a time the only sound was their own quickened breathing.

Eventually, she ended the kiss and leaned back to look into his eyes. "Thank you for being here. It's the best Christmas present ever," she said.

He slowed raised his hand and cupped her face. Tilting her chin back, he leaned down and, as their lips met again, put all his feelings for her into a long, tender kiss. Afterward, he wrapped his arms around her as her now familiar form melded against his. Her face turned into him, and her breath gently tickled his neck. "Merry Christmas, Lily."

"Merry Christmas, Ammon."

They stayed that way for some time and then, in unspoken accord, walked through the doorway into the kitchen. Lily impressed Ammon by staying fairly coherent during the making and baking of the cinnamon rolls.

They took their finished breakfast into the living room and ate by the light of the Christmas tree. It was only after they had eaten their frosting-smothered confections that Lily began falling asleep on the couch.

"You should go to bed, Lil. I can come back later," he promised.

"No," she murmured petulantly. "I want to be with you all day today."

"But you're falling asleep," he chuckled.

"Maybe I can just rest my head on your shoulder for a little while, and then I'll be good as new," she implored, looking up at him with big eyes.

Laughing, he arranged himself so she could better reach his shoulder. She curled into him and, in only a few minutes, was completely asleep. He hesitated for a moment then, reaching out with his right arm, gently caressed her cheek. He saw her smile unconsciously. His left arm tightened around her waist, and he touched her face again before resting his head on top of hers. For the first time in a long time, he felt at peace.

*****

Several hours later, Lily slowly regained consciousness. The first thing she realized was that her head rested on a pillow and a blanket covered her. Slowly sitting up, she noticed that sunlight streamed through the front window and the aroma of cooking ham laced the air. Furrowing her brow, Lily stretched her arms over her head and rotated her head around to fix the slight kink she had. She didn't remember putting the ham in the oven before falling asleep.

"Finally awake, sleepyhead?" she heard a voice tease. *That's right, Ammon is here!* Lily turned toward the doorway to the kitchen and saw Ammon leaning against the frame, spatula in hand and a smile on his face.

She smiled back. "How come you're up and about?"

"Well, I figured we couldn't both have a lazy day. Someone needed to slave away and cook up this delicious dinner you had waiting in the fridge."

"How long have I been asleep?"

"About five hours."

"Oh no! I left you alone for five hours," Lily moaned, putting her face in her hands. "I'm so sorry. I just meant to take a quick nap."

"It's fine, Lily, really." Ammon walked over and placed a quick kiss on top of her head. "I called my parents and talked with them for a while and then started cooking the dinner. It's no problem."

She looked up through her fingers. He looked cheerful enough, so he must be telling the truth. "In that case," Lily said slyly, "is dinner ready? I'm starving."

Ammon burst out laughing and reached down to pull her to her feet. "This way, Your Highness," he jested, leading her into the kitchen.

"Watch it. That nickname is already reserved for Kate," Lily joked.

They bantered back and forth as they completed their Christmas meal preparations. Before work yesterday, Lily prepared fruit salad, potato rolls, and an apple pie. To these, Ammon added deviled eggs and a green bean casserole. The meal was large for two people but, after saying grace, they dug into the food with gusto, determined to at least make a dent in it. Ammon shared more stories about his latest travels, and Lily filled him in on some of her more interesting work experiences. Happily for her, Ammon didn't get queasy talking about hospital stories while eating. Her parents and siblings had long since banned her from speaking about anything medical over dinner.

"Okay." Lily sat back rubbing her stomach. "I give up. I'm full."

"I'm glad," said Ammon as he pushed away his plate, "because there's no way I can keep up if we go for thirds."

They stood and cleared the dishes, put the leftovers away, and walked back into the living room. They had lingered over dinner late into the afternoon. They were fortunate enough to see a beautiful sunset gracing the sky as they looked through the front window.

Lily walked to the window to better see the view, and Ammon came up behind her and wrapped his arms around her waist. She leaned back into him, and a peaceful silence descended as they both looked toward the heavens.

"Gorgeous," Lily sighed as the colors faded to blues and grays.

"Yes, you are," Ammon breathed in her ear.

Chuckling Lily said, "I meant the sunset."

"I know. But you're a beautiful woman, Lily, and I don't think you've been told that enough. So I'm going to keep saying it until you believe me."

Lily felt a little embarrassed but knew Ammon meant what he said. He was right; no man had ever admired her looks enough to say she was pretty, let alone beautiful. It felt strange to hear a compliment about her appearance, outside of how tall she was. People usually just told her she was smart or intimidating, never pretty.

"I'll work on believing you then," she replied with a shy smile.

"Good. Now take a minute and call your family. After you're done, we could finish off our Christmas celebrations with a game or a puzzle."

"You always know the right thing to say." Lily laughed.

Lily had actually called her parents briefly on her way home from work that morning to wish them merry Christmas. They were always up with the sun, and Lily knew she wouldn't be waking them by calling so early. Her parents laughingly told her that they were the only ones awake, however. Will, Kate, and Jack were taking full advantage of the holidays and sleeping in. Lucky for her, Will and Kate were down in Arizona for the holidays, so she didn't have to come up with an excuse for not seeing them after her shift.

She sat on the couch and dialed her parents' home number while Ammon went to pick out an activity. She spent some time happily listening to the Christmas happenings in her parents' home. She said a hello to Jack, who'd recently returned from his study abroad, and made some plans to see him when he came back up to school for the next semester. She also promised to call Kate and chat with her longer another day.

When she finished, Lily joined Ammon at the dining table. They spent the rest of the evening putting together a puzzle featuring Santa's workshop, eating pie, and singing Christmas songs. At the close of the night, Ammon wrapped his arms around Lily for a long hug. Before releasing her, he whispered, "Good night, my fair Lily."

"Good night, Ammon. Thank you for an amazing Christmas."

She tilted her head as he leaned in for a goodbye kiss, and then he stepped out into the snow. As he walked quickly to his car, Lily noticed the shoveled sidewalk and realized he must have done that too while she slept. He really was so thoughtful.

She still didn't feel like she deserved him, but perhaps if he stuck around a little longer, this fairy-tale story might start feeling real.

17
chapter

A couple weeks into January, Kate called Lily and invited her over to dinner. She had only seen Kate a handful of times over the last few months, mostly because she had been so busy with Ammon. "I feel like we haven't seen you in forever, Lil," Kate said. "You've been so busy with your work, and we've been distracted by Will's job. It just feels like we need to get together and play catch up."

"I'd love to!" Lily exclaimed. "What day did you have in mind?"

"Are you working tomorrow night?"

"Nope. I'm totally free."

"That's great. Will thought we might invite Ammon too, if that's okay with you."

"Ammon's out of town," Lily responded without thinking.

She heard Kate pause and then slowly say, "Why do you know that?"

Uh-oh, Lily thought. Telling Will and Kate about her relationship with Ammon was inevitable, though she hadn't planned on telling them quite yet. She was waiting until she felt confident it would last; sometime around the day of her wedding seemed more appropriate. Still, she supposed she couldn't hide it from them any longer.

"It's a long story. Can I tell you tomorrow?"

"I'll be waiting on pins and needles until then."

The next evening, Lily arrived at Will's apartment and took a deep breath before knocking on the door. To her surprise, Will opened the door. He folded his arms across his chest and regarded her with a raised eyebrow.

Lily squirmed under the scrutiny and then said, "How's it going, Will?"

"How's it going?" he repeated sarcastically. "Really, Lil? Is that all the thanks I get for introducing you to Ammon and enabling you to be whatever it is that you two are? The least you could do is start groveling at my feet and singing my endless praises."

Lily looked at his face and noticed his stern posture relaxing as he started laughing. "Jerk." Lily chuckled as she pushed past him through the door and into the front room.

"Seriously though, Kate told me you knew Ammon was out of town before I did. What's going on with you two? I didn't even know you'd talked since we brought him over. Neither of you said a word about it. How long has this been going on?"

"Well, it's hard to say exactly," Lily hedged. "He called a few weeks after that dinner, and we've seen each other fairly often since then I suppose."

"What do you mean by fairly often?" Kate questioned as she emerged from the kitchen. Lily knew the look on her face spelled trouble. Kate stared at her with her piercing gaze until Lily had to look away. There was no way to hide anything from Kate when she looked like that. "Lily. Spill it. Now."

Kate sounded so intense that Lily was taken by surprise. She knew she would get a lot of grief from Will over not telling him about seeing Ammon, but she didn't think Kate would mind so much. On the other hand, Lily usually told Kate everything. Maybe she should have let her in on her secret sooner; Kate seemed hurt.

"Oh, Kate," Lily began, "I didn't mean to keep a secret for so long. I just didn't know where it was going, and I didn't want to jinx it. And I knew if Will found out then I'd never hear the end of it."

"Wait," Will interrupted, looking confused. "Are you saying you're dating? I just thought you guys were hanging out as friends."

Lily gulped. Truth time. "We are dating. I think," she replied. Come to think of it, they had never exactly sat down and decided what they were. She never liked the idea of defining a relationship and figured once she started kissing someone, they were dating exclusively. Did Ammon feel the same way?

She forgot she was answering Will and Kate and started thinking about all the conversations she had ever had with Ammon. Not one time did he refer to her as his girlfriend. Of course, she never really referred to him as her boyfriend. Though that was probably because she hadn't told anyone she was even seeing him. Was she his girlfriend?

"Lily?" Kate prompted.

"Hmm?"

"Are you okay?"

Now Kate appeared concerned. Lily couldn't decide what she felt now. She had felt so over the moon to be spending time with Ammon, she hadn't even thought about how he saw things. She wondered if she should ask him whether or not he had changed his mind about being in a serious relationship. Should she ask him what his intentions were? That sounded so serious, and yet she didn't want to be hoping for something long-term if he hadn't changed his mind about being with someone. But then why was he spending time with her? He wouldn't have kissed her, and kept kissing her, if he didn't want to serious date her. At least, she hoped not.

"Lily," Will said, interrupting her runaway thoughts, "do you know what you're doing? I mean, do you know about Ammon's past? Has he told you anything about Laura?"

"He told me about her the first time we were together. He told me about his stance on relationships too," Lily replied.

"So, has that changed?" Will questioned.

"I…um, I guess we haven't really talked about it like that."

"Lil, I'm not generally one to give relationship advice," Will stated, "but I do know Ammon. When he makes a commitment to something, he doesn't usually change his mind. Now, I personally think his decision to not date again was asinine, so I totally support your seeing him. I just don't want to see you get hurt if you haven't really thought this through."

"I wouldn't have thought you'd know the word asinine," Lily joked weakly. This conversation was not going as planned, and now all she wanted to do was talk about anything else.

"Lil," Kate said with a sad smile on her face, "don't change the subject. We just don't want to see you get hurt. We love you so much, and we love Ammon too. We'd be over the moon if you ended up together." She held up a hand to Will, who seemed about to protest.

"Yes, we would. Will's always said that Ammon deserves someone amazing, and you are amazing."

"And maybe we're blowing this out of proportion," Will added. "I mean, how much are you seeing him really? It's not like you're exclusively dating him, is it?"

Lily bit her lip and looked away. Apparently, that was enough for Kate to figure things out.

"You're kissing him, aren't you?" Kate asked. Kate knew that, to Lily, even just kissing someone was serious.

"Wait, what?" Will stuttered. "You're not, right? Tell her you're not."

Lily opened her mouth to explain and then closed it. What an awkward thing to be discussing with her brother. As much as she loved Will, this was definitely not something she felt comfortable sharing with him. She looked at Kate for help.

"Will," Kate said, seeing Lily's silent plea, "could you go check on the chicken please?"

Will was staring at Lily as if willing her to say something to refute the kissing allegations, but after a moment he turned and went into the kitchen. Kate watched him go, then turned to Lily.

"Are you sure?"

Was she sure? She knew that the way she felt about Ammon surpassed anything she had ever felt for another man. She knew that without him she would feel broken and lost. She knew that he lit up her world. She knew he cared about her. She knew she had fallen in love with him.

"Yes."

"Well then, I'm happy for you both." Kate smiled.

Lily felt relieved that Kate left it at that. Now, however, she knew she needed to find answers to the questions she hadn't voiced before. As much as it scared her, she knew she needed to know if Ammon really wanted to be with her. She desperately hoped so, because she already couldn't imagine life without him.

18

chapter

Lily laced up her running shoes and donned her jacket before making her way outside. It was the end of January and still too icy to run outside, so she planned to hit up a treadmill at the gym near her house before work.

Ammon came home tonight. She had seen him a few times this month, though his work schedule had kept him out of state, mostly out of the country in fact since Christmas. She still hadn't gotten up the courage to ask him about their relationship. Every time she saw him, she was so grateful for the time they had together, she feared bringing up something so serious. And what if he didn't want her? She wasn't ready to face that thought either.

But the dinner at Will's kept haunting her. They had made it through the night, if somewhat awkwardly. Will would glance at her as if trying to figure out what she hadn't told him, which made her squirm and long to get away. But she didn't want to hurt Kate more than she already had by not being forthcoming about Ammon. So she made herself stay as long as she could to talk with her.

Speaking of which, she felt like Kate was hiding something herself. There was a seriousness to her that wasn't normally present. When Lily asked about her plans for this next year, she felt like Kate's answers were a little elusive. She didn't want to pry, however. She knew how it felt to keep a secret.

A few sweaty miles later, Lily slowed to a walk to cool down. She had made up her mind during her run to ask Ammon about his feelings. Her heart raced at the thought. What if he didn't want her?

She thought that again and again. She still couldn't believe he felt attracted to her in the first place.

She kept trying to tell herself that everything would be fine, but deep down she knew that this conversation might just shatter all her hopes and dreams. She hoped she was brave enough to handle whatever Ammon might say. She also desperately hoped that he would say he wanted her.

*****

Ammon threw his coat on the bed and then landed heavily on top of it. His latest round of assignments had wiped him out completely. He closed his eyes and laid his arms across his chest. He could fall asleep right now and be out for twelve hours easily if he wanted to.

With a sigh, however, he reluctantly got up and headed for his editing computer. His boss wanted his pictures sent over as soon as possible, so he knew he needed to get started now. He also knew that if he did it tonight, he would feel less guilty spending time tomorrow with Lily instead of working.

Speaking of Lily, Ammon reached for his phone. He knew she worked tonight, but she usually tried to send him a message whenever she had a moment between patients. He looked as he sat at his computer and didn't see a message from Lily. Instead, he saw one from Will.

He felt a little guilty thinking about Will. He kept avoiding telling him about his relationship with Lily, because he wasn't sure that Will would approve. Ammon knew Will loved Lily and was very protective of her, despite his constant teasing. Will had known Ammon long enough to know he wasn't perfect, far from it in fact, but they still had a great friendship. Will was the only one who'd really seen how deeply Laura's leaving had affected him. Will had been instrumental in getting him through some really dark times. He only hoped Will would overlook his shortcomings and be happy when he found out he was seeing Lily.

Opening the message, he felt surprised at what it said. "If you are kissing my sister, you better be serious about being with her. If you break her heart, I'll break your legs. Let me know when you're back, and we'll have you over for dinner."

Ammon gave an amused grunt at the typical Will-style message—inviting someone over after threatening bodily harm. With a sigh, Ammon closed the phone and looked up at the ceiling. So somehow Will knew that he was seeing Lily. He would have told Will eventually; he just wasn't planning on doing it quite yet. He had been hoping to wait until he knew where things would go with her.

It wasn't that he was ashamed to be seen with Lily. She was such a good, talented, and beautiful person that he half wanted to shout to the world that she was with him. However, he still felt uncomfortable being vulnerable with someone. As much as he enjoyed being around her, he'd never really let her see the injured side of him. He'd told her about Laura and his vow to stay single, but that was as close as he got to allowing her to see his hurt. His pride feared her reaction if she discovered how deeply broken he was. He didn't want to risk opening himself up again just to see her walk away.

He wished he didn't have to think about the future. He wanted it to be enough to live in the moment, but he knew that couldn't last forever. It amazed him that Lily hadn't already asked him again about his vow to stay single, especially after he'd kissed her. Of course, since he'd initiated that kiss, perhaps she had assumed he had changed his mind.

He wished that he felt comfortable moving forward. He knew Lily's personality to be caring and kind. It's what made her such a great nurse. He toyed with the idea of showing her his weaknesses and hurts, but he feared he would see pity in her eyes and that was more than he could bear. He knew he wasn't good enough to be with her, and he didn't want to drag her into something that would dim her light. The part of him still resisting a permanent relationship told him to leave before he ruined them both.

Ammon sighed and leaned back in his chair. He didn't feel ready to make this decision, but he knew that it was time to figure out what he wanted to happen with Lily.

*****

For the first time in months, Lily found herself feeling nervous about seeing Ammon. She usually felt a giddy excitement that transformed into complete happiness when Ammon came home from his latest assignment. Today she felt like her stomach was tied in knots. She had spent the entire shift last night talking herself into asking him about their relationship, but she still felt like she might lose her nerve.

She didn't sleep well, so midday she gave up and walked over to his house. She found herself on his porch without remembering exactly how she got there. As she raised her hand to knock, she noticed it was shaking. She closed her eyes, took a deep breath, and after a few brief knocks, opened the door and walked inside.

Ammon came out of his room and walked quickly over to where she stood. Seeing his welcoming smile made some of the nervousness fade, and Lily berated herself for feeling anxious about coming over. As he took her in his arms and gave her a big hug, she felt herself relaxing against him. It felt like coming home.

"Lily," Ammon said into her hair, "I missed you."

She turned her face up toward his and was rewarded with a warm, lingering kiss. She began wondering why she had ever worried about his feelings. She felt herself smiling against his lips.

Ammon pulled back slightly, noticed her smile, and said, "Feeling happy today?"

"I am now," she answered. "I missed you too. How was your assignment?"

Ammon started filling her in on the details while he led her over to the couch. They sat down, and he held her hand for a few minutes before starting to caress her arm lightly. She lost herself in that warm sensation for several minutes until he mentioned getting a text from Will.

She looked quickly at him. Was it her imagination or did he look uncomfortable for a moment? "What did it say?"

"He invited me over for dinner sometime," Ammon said, looking away.

Lily frowned. That couldn't have been all it said, otherwise Ammon wouldn't look so uneasy. "Did Will say something about us?" she asked quietly. "I went over for dinner a couple of weeks ago, and we sort of came up."

"Did we? Will did mention something about bodily harm."

Lily put her head in her hands and groaned. "Please tell me Will's not trying to interfere?"

"Will is being a good older brother."

Lily looked up. Ammon was looking at her, but she couldn't quite decipher what he was feeling. His normally expressive eyes were shuttered. She didn't like the way that made her feel. He was hiding his true feelings, so he must feel uncomfortable with Will's message because it insinuated something that he didn't want. All her nervousness from earlier came flooding back, and she unconsciously pulled away from Ammon as her fears consumed her.

"Lily? Are you all right? I'm sorry. I didn't mean to make you feel bad. I'm sure he's only trying to protect you."

"I just," she took a deep breath and glanced away before continuing, "I just need to know if you want to be with me. If you want to keep seeing me as more than a friend."

There, she'd said it. She hesitated, gathering her courage to look at Ammon. After a few moments of silence, she turned back to him.

The look on his face could only be called indecision, and her heart fell. He didn't want her, but he didn't know how to tell her. She felt her eyes well up with tears but fought them down. She hated to cry in front of anyone, and she wasn't about to start now.

"You still don't know if you want to be in a romantic relationship with me," Lily whispered. Her heart broke just saying the words out loud. She took a deep breath and asked, "Do you want me to go?"

"No," Ammon responded immediately. "No, I want you to stay, Lily. But forgive me, I suppose that's part of the problem."

"The problem?"

"Oh, Lily, I'm not explaining very well. What I mean is, I like you. I enjoy being with you, holding you, and talking to you." He grabbed her hands and held them in his. He looked her straight in the eyes, and she could see that he was struggling to decide what he wanted. "Lily, more than anything I want to do what's right for you.

For both of us. There's still a part of me that's not sure if I can truly commit to anyone again. But if I could, it would be to you. I really like you, Lily. Please believe me."

Lily stayed silent for a few moments, feeling the warmth of his hands holding hers and wondering if she had the strength to hold on or, worse, to let them go. It seemed like either path would be a difficult one to walk.

"Do you," she paused, "do you need some time to decide? I mean, without me being here."

"Lily, I want you to stay, but only you know if that's what's right for you."

She thought about everything he'd said and everything he didn't say. He wasn't ready to commit to being with her, and yet he cared for her. She could feel it. She should probably walk away until he figured out what he wanted, but she didn't want to. She wanted to be here. Though she knew if she stayed, she would have to put some distance between them.

"This isn't how I planned on welcoming you home." She smiled sadly as she withdrew her hands. The gesture pained her, but she knew she couldn't be as affectionate as she wanted to right now. "I'll stay if that's okay, but it would be best if I kept a little distance, I think."

Ammon's smile mirrored her sadness, but he didn't contradict her. She wished he would. She ached for him to decide right then that she was what he wanted, but she knew his past demons still held sway over him.

"What were your plans for my homecoming?" Ammon asked after a moment.

"Well, I did intend on kicking your trash at ping-pong."

"What are we waiting for then?"

He automatically started to reach for her hand to help her up, but Lily saw him hesitate and then slowly drop his arm back to his side. With a sigh of sadness, she pushed herself off the couch and followed him to the ping-pong table. What in the world was she going to do now?

19
chapter

Ironically, Ammon didn't travel much the next two months, so they had plenty of time to spend together.

"Figures," Lily muttered to herself while walking to Ammon's. "We finally get to spend some quality time together, and we're not together. What am I doing?"

She asked that question every day. Ammon seemed to have easily slipped back into being just friends. Meanwhile, as much as Lily enjoyed all the activities they did together, she missed the physical part of their relationship immeasurably. She tried to not see him in a romantic light as he'd asked, but keeping her distance was killing her. She longed to hug him when she came over, hold his hand while they watched a movie, or kiss him good night when she left in the evening. Their friendship meant a great deal to her, but she wondered if she should be as consumed by it as she was. If Ammon never changed his mind, what was the point of continuing on like this when she could be spending the time looking for someone else?

Still, she knew why she kept going. She loved him. She'd never told him she felt that way, but she knew it motivated everything she did. She also knew it wasn't mentally or emotionally healthy for her, but she didn't want to give up on him. In all her years of searching, she'd never found anyone who matched her so well on both an intellectual and physical level.

Something one of her former roommates had said constantly popped into her head now: baby steps. They would make a joke about it while walking to school on cold, snowy days. Baby steps to the next light pole, baby steps to the next building, and so on.

Maybe that's what she needed to focus on now. Baby steps with their friendship, baby steps until Ammon had time to figure out his issues, and baby steps for her while she tried to decide what her own heart needed.

*****

Being just friends was killing him. Every time he saw Lily, he had to physically restrain himself from reaching for her. It would be the most natural gesture in the world to take her hand or throw his arm over her shoulder. However, he knew that if he started doing that again without knowing what he wanted, he would hurt her more than he already had.

He could see her hurt in her eyes, in the tenseness of her shoulders, and the way she wouldn't meet his gaze like she used to. Knowing that his actions were causing her pain made him feel awful. If he would have just controlled himself and not gotten physical, then maybe they could have just continued to be friends without all this baggage. However, he imagined he would have fallen for Lily without ever even touching her. She fit him like no one ever had before. She was special that way.

Even after everything he had done, she still went out of her way to make his birthday memorable. His birthday was the day after Valentine's Day. Ammon had a feeling she worked the night shift on Valentine's on purpose, but she still stopped by early in the morning on her way home with some cinnamon rolls she'd made before her shift. After she woke up that afternoon, they played laser tag in the snow at the park with Will, Kate, and her brother Jack, who had come back to school after the winter holidays. Then she took him out to dinner at the Indian restaurant they both loved, and they ate until they were full to bursting. Afterward, they went to the dollar theater and saw an edited version of *The King's Speech*.

Ammon thought about how adorable Lily was when she talked about that movie. The ending sequence had feature Lily's favorite Beethoven symphony along with King George's epic speech. He could see the depth of emotions on Lily's face as she watched, completely enraptured.

She had no idea how close he came in that moment to throwing all his talk of boundaries aside. He had wanted nothing more than to kiss her soundly in the middle of the theater. Seeing Lily so happy filled him with such joy that he hadn't wanted to lose that feeling again.

However, he'd let the moment pass, and so they were still in relationship limbo. He knew she was waiting for him to decide what he wanted, but he didn't know what to do. He still didn't want the vulnerability of a romantic attachment, but the thought of another man being with her made him ill.

All these thoughts passed through his mind while he paced through his house waiting for Lily. He knew she would be over shortly since they had made plans to go rock climbing together today at the indoor climbing gym in town.

Ammon smiled thinking about how their plans had come about. They had gone for a walk through the freshly fallen snow a few nights ago and passed several towering evergreen trees.

"Have you ever climbed one of those?" he asked, pointing.

"Can't say that I have. Their needles and branches are so pokey. Have you?"

"We used to do it all the time in New York. But we usually waited to climb them until the snow was a few feet deep. We'd get as close to the top as we could, and then we'd see how far we could make the tree bend over. Then we'd drop into the snow."

Lily looked aghast. "Are you crazy? Wouldn't that hurt?"

"No. The snow cushioned our fall. It was actually really fun."

"What did your mom have to say about that particular activity?"

"She just shook her head and told us she was glad we were still alive. Of course, we didn't tell her until just a few years ago. If she'd found out we were doing it when we were young, we'd have been so busted."

Ammon remembered how Lily had just shaken her head and chuckled at his boyhood antics. "Well," she had finally replied, "if you like climbing trees, you might like rock climbing. Have you ever tried it?"

"Not officially. I've messed around climbing around on boulders while hiking, but that's all. It sounds like fun."

Lily had told him how much she loved it, and he had wanted to see her happy again. He knew he would probably outclimb her. He figured he was a fair bit stronger than she was, even though she definitely wasn't soft. He didn't want to hurt her feelings though, so he would try and not show her up.

As he finished that thought, he passed a window and felt a smile start as he realized Lily was already here. She stood on the lawn, and she seemed to be speaking with someone. His eyes narrowed when he realized his neighbor, Bill, was flirting with her.

He shouldn't care, but he felt himself getting irritated with Bill. Bill should know that Lily was here for him. He quickly walked out the door and down his front steps before he could analyze his feelings too closely.

He walked over to Lily and stood closer to her than he probably should. Just so Bill would understand that Lily wasn't available. Of course, she was available since he insisted on not dating her, but Bill wasn't her type anyway.

Lily glanced at him out of the corner of her eye, and he caught the bemused look on her face. She'd likely guessed at his motives, but he would deal with that later. At least Bill seemed to understand the silent threat. He took one look at Ammon's face, hurriedly said his goodbyes to Lily, and walked back inside.

Ammon rejoiced in his minor victory but didn't let himself glory in it too long. Unless he decided to let go of his past, there would be a day when Lily walked away to another man and he would be powerless to stop her.

20

chapter

Ammon's first thought after walking through the doors to the climbing gym was that he was entering another dimension. Everywhere he looked there were fake colorful rock formations and different patterned pieces of tape dotting the walls. The evening crowd had not descended yet, but there was still a fair number of people steadily scaling the different walls.

He noticed one particular wall where the climbers seemed to not be tethered to a rope from the top. He looked more closely and realized the rope trailed beneath them as they made their way upward. How could that be safe?

"Lead climbing," Lily said. She must have noticed where he was looking. He glanced at her, and she seemed to understand his desire for more information.

"The climbers are tied into their ropes, and the person belaying them stands at the bottom and feeds them the rope as they make their way to the top. There are several anchors along the route, and, as they climb, they clip into those anchors to secure themselves to the wall. It's an advanced way to climb and definitely not for the faint of heart."

Her words proved prophetic for just then one of the climbers must have slipped, and he suddenly plummeted several feet toward the floor before he jerked to a stop, swinging on his now taut rope.

Ammon shook his head, and Lily let out a small laugh. "Yeah, that's not really my cup of tea," she said. "I prefer to top rope." She gestured toward the area of the gym where Ammon could see the ropes securely fastened to the top of the wall.

"I think I prefer to start that way as well," he replied.

"Well then, let's get your gear on and head down to the floor. We'll have to get you belay certified, but then we can head over there and look for some fun routes."

He figured what she said would make sense eventually, so he let himself go with the flow. As it turned out, being belay certified meant he was qualified to be the person on the other end of the rope from the climber. He needed to hold enough tension on the rope so that if the climber fell, he could quickly stop the fall. Lily also explained, however, that he needed to give her some slack so that she had some freedom of movement as she worked her route.

After they finished getting him certified to climb, Lily led Ammon over to a deserted section of the wall. "If you look closely, you can see that there are pieces of tape with different numbers and letters on them," Lily pointed out. "They all start with five, and then there is a period and another number. The lower the second number, the easier the route."

Ammon looked around and noticed that the lowest number was 5.5. But there were also several routes with letters attached. He called Lily's attention to those.

"Oh, the letters are to give a grade of difficulty within the second number. An *a* would be the easiest, and a *d* would be the hardest. I've managed to work up to doing 5.11c's, but that's as good as I've gotten so far. I prefer bigger movements like chimneys, and once you're in the 11's it feels like most everything is really crimpy."

Ammon just looked at her with a raised eyebrow. Lily burst out laughing. "I guess the lingo does take some getting used to." She smiled. "Let's start out on a 5.8 just to get warmed up."

"Sounds good to me, but maybe you better go first." Ammon smiled back.

Lily put her shoes on with a grin, tied and checked her knot, then made sure Ammon had tied into the belay device correctly. Once she finished her checks, she walked over to the wall. He saw her look up for a moment and her hands moved, like she was miming the moves she would make.

"You always start where the tape has two pieces pointing toward a certain rock like this," she gestured to the rock in front of her. Sure enough, the tape made an arrow to the starting rock. "If there are two different holds to start on," she continued, "then there'll be two arrows."

She placed her hands on the rocks and looked back at him. "Ready?"

"Ready."

And then she started to climb. Ammon revised his opinion of his ability to outclimb Lily. Even though she'd said it was an easier route, he still found himself mesmerized as she fluidly moved from one handhold to the next. It seemed like she melded into the wall as she climbed. Before he knew it, she had made it to the top, and he had to shake himself slightly before repelling her to the ground.

"Are you ready to give it a go?" she asked after she loosened herself from the rope. She was flushed slightly, with either excitement or exertion he couldn't quite tell. She was beautiful.

"Bring it on," he said as he moved to repeat the route she'd just finished. He noticed Lily kicking off her shoes before tying into the belay. He raised another eyebrow.

"Free the feet," she quipped. "Seriously, though, the best climbing shoes are ones that are a few sizes smaller than you'd normally wear. Works great on the wall, but it kills my feet just to stand around in them."

"That makes sense if you're using your feet to help grip the wall," Ammon said, thinking out loud.

"You got it. Helpful on the wall, *hurty* on the ground."

Ammon laughed and finished tying himself into the rope. Lily checked his knot then gave him the go-ahead to climb. Time to see if he could keep up with his fair Lily.

*****

A couple of hours later, Lily looked over at Ammon and started giggling. His pain-filled expression turned toward her, and her giggles turned into outright laughter. She suspected he had thought he would be better at this than her. She knew she had surprised him with her abilities, and that thought made her day.

"Achy arms?" she asked when her laughter subsided.

"My forearms are killing me," Ammon admitted as he tried to rub them. "I want to rub them to try and work out some of the soreness, but my hands won't grip anything anymore."

Lily laughed again. She finished removing her harness, placed her gear in her bag, and walked over to where Ammon was trying in vain to loosen his harness. "I remember the first time I went climbing," she said as she started working his harness loose. "An old roommate met me here. After just an hour or so, I could barely get my fingers to work to open my car door. Climbing seems to work muscles that don't generally get used so intensely."

She finished loosening his harness. He stepped out of it, and she walked it over to the front counter to turn it back in. "I'll have to talk you into buying some equipment of your own so you don't have to rent every time you come with me," she said as she walked back over to Ammon.

Ammon moaned as he kept rubbing his arms. "You think you can talk me into this torture again?"

"Admit it, you had a great time."

"True enough," he said. "Though I didn't think you were stronger than me. How'd you outclimb me like that?"

"It's all about using your legs and positioning yourself on the wall so that you're not relying on just your upper body." Lily gestured toward Ammon's arms. "You're so sore because you thought you could just use your arms to pull yourself up. But perhaps I'll take pity on you, just this once. This was my idea after all." Lily reached out and started massaging Ammon's arms. She felt him stiffen but decided to ignore it. She was tired of keeping her distance and, besides, this was something she would do for anyone. What did it matter that her heart started racing as soon as she touched him?

After a moment, Ammon relaxed and Lily chanced looking up at him. She saw the usual warmth and desire, but the ever-present reluctance was there as well. With a sigh, she dropped her hands and turned to grab her bag.

"Well, we'll just have to come again so I can try some of the techniques that you use," Ammon said. "I don't think I want to do it again tomorrow, though. I'm pretty sure my arms are going to be sore for a few days. Maybe we could just play some ping-pong instead."

"Um, tomorrow?" Lily hesitated. This was going to be awkward, so she might as well just say it. "I actually have a date."

"What?"

"A date," she repeated as she turned back around to look at him. He looked stunned.

A few nights ago, her coworker had surprised her by asking if she could set Lily up with her son. Lily could have sworn everyone knew the story of Ammon's appearance on the unit at Christmas. At least, she now got asked about her love life far more often than she liked.

Somehow the rumor mill hadn't reached Dawn. Apparently, her son had tickets to a soccer match but his original date fell through. Dawn told Trixie about the situation while they were working one night, and Trix nominated her as a good substitute. When Dawn approached her and asked if she would go on a last-minute blind date, Lily reluctantly agreed. Now she was glad she had accepted.

She lifted her bag onto her shoulder and prepared to leave. When she saw Ammon hadn't moved, she sighed, walked over, and squeezed his hand. "Ready to go? I'm thinking we deserve some ice cream after that workout."

"Um, yeah. Ice cream would be good," Ammon replied slowly, still studying her.

"Great. Let's go." Lily gave Ammon's hand a tug and then released it when he started slowly walking with her out to the car. Yes indeed, this might work in her favor after all.

21
chapter

Lily was on a date. Right now. With someone else.

Ammon groaned into his hands as he sank further into the couch in the game room. The ping-pong table mocked him from the corner, reminding him again that Lily wasn't here. Thinking of her on a date was as painful now as it had been last night when she'd told him of her plans. He knew he didn't have a right to dictate her life or how she spent her time, but he wished with all his soul that she was here with him right now.

Instead, someone else was enjoying her smiles, her laugh, and her witty conversation. Would that other guy be wise enough to understand how lucky he was to be spending time with Lily? The worst part was that Ammon had only himself to blame. If he could just open himself up completely to Lily, then they could move forward in their relationship. He knew that she was interested in him, and even after all the things he'd done, he hadn't managed to drive her away.

Even though theirs was just a friendship right now, Ammon knew that Lily cared for him, and he thought she would be willing to give a romantic relationship with him another chance. She wasn't like other women from his past who were flighty and unreliable. Lily was the one constant in his life these last several months. It didn't matter where his job took him or for how long, she'd always been willing to continue talking and sharing her thoughts with him. She'd stayed true to her promise to be friends.

Now he could see, however, that he had not been as constant in his desire for mere friendship. Though he'd never resumed kissing her, there were some days when he'd stood closer than he should or looked at her with feelings of more than friendship evident in his eyes. She must wonder every day what version of him she was getting—whether it was the Ammon that kept her at arm's length or the Ammon that wanted more.

If she felt at all like he did, he wondered how in the world she had dealt with her emotions all this time, because after just one day of not having Lily around, he felt worried and anxious. He hated not knowing whether she was happier with someone else than she was with him. He didn't like it. He wanted her in his life, and he wanted her to be his. It finally dawned on him that it wasn't romantic celibacy that would keep him from feeling vulnerable, it was trusting the right person. It was trusting Lily, the woman that he loved.

He couldn't believe it had taken him all this time to see what was so clearly right in front of his face. He loved her. He loved everything about her, but most especially he loved her kind heart. Who else would have put up with his crazy relationship issues without either throwing it back in his face or walking away? She saw something in him worth fighting for, and that thought changed how he felt about everything, especially himself.

His heart started beating faster as he realized where his thoughts were leading him. He didn't know how long she would make him apologize before she was willing to give him another chance to win her, but he knew that time didn't matter now. He would do whatever it took, for however long it took, to convince her that he had made up his mind. She was more important to him than he even knew how to express.

Ammon got off the couch and started pacing the room. The possibilities of a future with Lily made him feel almost giddy. He didn't want her for just a little while. He wanted her forever. Would she think he was crazy if he proposed? Probably better rein that thought in for a little while, but it was where he wanted things to go now that he finally had his head on straight.

He looked at his watch. It was nearly ten o'clock. He knew the soccer match started at seven, so it must be over by now. He imagined that Lily would be arriving home soon. He couldn't wait to see her. He didn't even care if her date saw him sitting on the porch waiting for her to get home.

He laughed out loud. The sight of him striding over, letting Lily out of the car, and then kissing her soundly should put to rest any aspirations of a second date. He probably shouldn't do it, but he couldn't help grinning at the idea. If he left now, he could be over to Lily's in five minutes.

Ammon strode into his room to get ready. A quick glance in the mirror of his bathroom showed a face resolute and truly happy for the first time in months. He grabbed his coat and keys and headed down the hall.

As he passed the game room, he heard a knock on the door. His face split into a huge grin. Lily had come after her date. He thought of sweeping her off her feet into an enormous hug and just holding her for hours.

His steps slowed slightly as he realized the front door remained closed. Lily never waited for an invitation to enter. She just walked in. His grin changed to puzzlement as he continued his walk to the door. Who in the world would be visiting this late at night except for Lily?

He grasped the knob and opened the door. All of the air in his lungs fled out in a rush. He couldn't breathe. This couldn't be happening. Not now.

"Are you going to invite me in out of the cold, handsome?" the woman asked.

He blinked, but she was still there. This had to be a bad dream. Her head cocked, and she started to grin as she looked at him. "Laura."

22
chapter

Lily sat in her front yard, methodically pulling weeds out of the grass. Weeding was something she did when she was worried or stressed. It helped her feel like she was accomplishing something. She'd done a lot of weeding the last few days.

It was the end of March, and things were just starting to warm up enough to grow. The green of new leaves and returning grass spread across her yard, and as she turned her head east, she could see the mountains beginning to emerge from their snowy sleep. Lily loved spring; it was her favorite season. But this year, spring didn't bring the renewal of energy and life she usually felt. Though the noon sun warmed her face, inside she felt cold and wary.

Her date the other night had been typical for her, uncomfortable and not worth a repeat performance. She'd enjoyed the soccer match, though. Maybe Ammon would want to go to one with her. The season was just beginning, so there would be plenty of chances to find one that fits into his schedule.

She sighed, thinking about Ammon. She hadn't heard from him since they'd gone climbing the other night. Perhaps, he liked the idea of her dating other people and was putting some distance between them so she didn't feel awkward about pursuing other men. She hoped that wasn't the case. She'd gone out of sympathy for her coworker, though a small part of her had hoped that knowing she was going out with other people would encourage Ammon to want to take her out again himself.

She'd also wanted to see if she could feel a romantic attraction to another man, but she hadn't felt a single spark of interest on her date. All she could do was compare him with Ammon. She'd missed Ammon's company all night long, though she'd tried to at least make the date as pleasant as she could. She wondered what Ammon had done while she was out, and she wondered if he'd thought of her. She'd hoped he would seek out her company again, but after not hearing from him for a few days, she couldn't help but think that he hadn't missed her at all.

She took a breath to get her runaway emotions under control and glanced up to find a new patch of weeds. As she did so, her eyes caught a glimpse of a familiar form slowly walking down the sidewalk toward her. Her heart began to race as she stood, brushing the dirt from her hands and jeans as well as she could.

Lily's nervousness increased as she continued to watch him move toward her. He looked heavy, as if the weight of the world had dropped directly onto his shoulders. He'd been that way the first time she met him, and she wondered with dread what made him appear that way again now. Her hands slowly clenched into fists at her side as fear overcame all other thought.

He raised his head as he neared her house and finally noticed her standing in the yard, watching him. His steps slowed for a moment, and then his pace resumed. He didn't rush to see her, she noticed. Fear on top of fear now.

"Lily."

"Hello, Ammon." She waited while he slowly finished crossing her yard and stood in front of her. His hands stayed in his pockets, and his body tense.

Her stomach clenched, but she gathered her courage. "Would you like to come inside, or we could head into the backyard and relax in the camping hammocks?" She waited with bated breath, hoping that whatever gloom hung over him, it wouldn't have anything to do with his relationship with her.

Finally, Ammon looked directly at her, and her breath fled from her lungs. His eyes. They'd become the glaciers they'd always reminded her of. What in the world had happened?

"Lily, I can't stay long. I just came to say goodbye."

Goodbye. Despite her intentions to be stoic in front of him, her eyes began to well up with tears. Her legs shook, and she consciously forced herself to breathe and remain upright. Trying to wrap her mind around this sudden change, she asked the only question she could. "Why?"

"I'm not being fair to you. I'm not good enough for you, Lily. I want you to have someone in your life that can care for you the way you deserve. Being with me is just getting in your way."

Lily was gasping for air now but trying not to let him see it. She understood the words coming out of his mouth, but they didn't make sense. Even if he didn't want to date her, why cut off their friendship? What made him so uncomfortable that he had to leave her completely? Didn't he know how she felt about him?

"But I love you." She hadn't meant to say it out loud, but her scattered brain had found a center in that thought, and it seemed to slip out without conscious effort.

Ammon looked pained. His body stiffened, and he took a deep breath as he looked down. "I can't love you. I'm sorry." He looked as though he thought about saying more, but instead he shook his head slowly and turned away.

Lily felt her hand begin to reach for him, as if she could hold him back from leaving. Perhaps, if they talked it through, she would understand why he felt he had to leave. What had she done that made him want to walk away?

"Ammon, please," Lily whispered.

"Lily," Ammon said without turning around. He sighed and shook his head again. "It's better this way."

Lily watched him walk away. No words emerged from her, though after a while she noticed, somewhat disjointedly, that her hand still reached out toward where he'd stood. But he was gone now, and she couldn't see him ever coming back.

23
chapter

"Lily? I asked if you wanted to come to the *Harry Potter*—themed birthday party I'm throwing for Jack," Kate repeated as she finished pulling off her harness. "It's on a Friday, which I know you have off, so no excuses for not coming because of work."

Lily shook herself out of her daydream. As usual, it involved Ammon. The memories of going climbing with him four months ago had taken over while she'd been here with Kate. It seemed the memories often got the best of her.

"Um," Lily hesitated as she tried to find a way out of going. It wasn't that she didn't love Jack and *Harry Potter*, but even after all these months, she still wasn't happy. It was hard to hide her feelings of melancholy from her family. She hated the questions and, worse, the well-meant advice to move on.

Jack's twenty-fifth birthday was July 31, and after being on a study abroad in England, he had discovered a love of the English-born hero. Lily knew that she would normally be just as excited as Kate about throwing a Harry-themed party, but lately nothing seemed to snap her out of her gloom. She was depressed, she knew it, and frankly she didn't care about fixing it right now. She just wanted to feel miserable. She missed Ammon, but she also missed who she was with him.

"Lily. Look at me right now."

Uh-oh. Kate's no-nonsense voice didn't come out very often, but when it did, Lily knew she was in trouble. Reluctantly, preparing for the inevitable lecture, she looked at Kate.

"Lily, I love you so much. Have you forgotten who you are? You are more than a broken relationship. You are my friend, you are my sister, and I miss you."

Lily's eyes widened in surprise. Kate's words were not what she expected. Something inside of her broke a little listening to them. For the first time in months, some emotion seemed to trickle into the void inside her.

"How can you miss me?" Lily's voice shook a little, and she cleared her throat. "I've been here the whole time."

"Your body has perhaps, but your mind and your spirit live in the past. You stopped living the day Ammon walked out of your life."

Lily winced. Trust Kate to put it bluntly, but she was right. Lily kept functioning because she had to, but the joy she felt before Ammon left was all but gone now. Even before he'd entered her life, she had found happiness in so many things. Now, nothing pulled at her. Even things she loved doing before had become gray and lifeless.

"I just want you to know that whenever you feel like you want to come back, I'm here for you. I won't push you. I won't tell you your feelings should change right now, but I want you to know that I'll be waiting. And I'll always be here to listen."

Those words, more than any other admonition she had received, made her feel the tiniest spark of hope that perhaps she wouldn't feel this way forever. That was an encouraging thought. With a hope born of another's love, Lily decided she would make a step in a positive direction. "Thanks, Kate. I'll be there for the party, and I'll bring the butterbeer."

*****

Jack's party was in full swing. Several of his friends from school and church stood chatting in groups throughout Will's house and backyard. Kate buzzed around the kitchen, pulling hot appetizers from the oven and placing them on the buffet set up in the kitchen. The whole party had an otherworldly feel as one of the prerequisites for attending was Hogwarts robes and wands.

Lily's own Ravenclaw-emblemed ensemble matched Jack's, and she waved at him across the room as he floated from one group to the next. She'd given herself the assignment of helping keep food on the buffet and butterbeer flowing in the drink fountain. It made her heart happy to see him looking so animated and alive.

Ever since her talk with Kate, she felt like small pieces of her personality were slowly creeping back into her life. She wasn't the same person as she had been before meeting Ammon, and his presence and now absence in her life had definitely left a mark. Those first few months after he'd left were the darkest times in her life. She'd been completely lost and despondent. Now, after her talk with Kate, she felt a small desire to find herself again. It would take a long time before she felt more normal, but at least she wasn't as hopeless as before.

Lily felt a pang thinking about Ammon, as she always did, but this time she didn't dwell on it. Instead, she purposefully turned her thoughts to the party and the reason she was here. She wanted Jack to have a fun night, and she wanted herself to have a good night too.

"It's a great turnout, isn't it?" Will commented as he joined Lily. He placed a tray of treacle tarts on the buffet, and Lily smiled.

"Have you been enlisted?" she teased.

"Lily, one day you'll learn that when you get married, you're already enlisted in everything your spouse wants you to do. You just don't know it yet." He placed an arm over her shoulders and started scanning the crowd.

Lily felt her insides squeeze a little at the reference to marriage, but she knew Will wasn't trying to pressure her to move on. He probably didn't have a clue as to how much she missed Ammon, and she certainly wasn't going to bring it up now.

Lily remembered the first time she saw Will and Kate after Ammon left. It had been over a week later, but Lily still recalled how shocked and numb she felt. She was heartbroken that, despite confessing that she loved him, Ammon had still walked away. It seemed like all the color in her world had left with him, and everything was gray. She hadn't reached out to anyone, not knowing how to describe what had happened and knowing she didn't want to pretend that she was okay. She had come over for dinner because she couldn't say no to Kate's request. Once there, it didn't take long for them to notice she came alone.

She hadn't meant to tell them any of the details of what had transpired, but she found herself mentioning that she had told Ammon she loved him, but he hadn't returned her feelings. She could see the thunder clouds forming on Will's face when she explained that Ammon was now no longer a part of her life. As much as Kate was there to listen when she had problems, Will was there to physically destroy whoever caused Lily pain. Still, she had no desire for Will to try and injure Ammon, and truthfully, she didn't feel angry at Ammon for what he'd said. So in an effort to keep everyone's limbs intact, she intentionally made it sound like it had been a mutual decision.

Even so, Will somehow knew that Lily was still hurting, and it definitely brought out the overprotective brother instincts. It touched her to see how much he cared. Her family was truly wonderful, and she felt grateful that she could always rely on them to be there for her.

Will stayed close to Lily all evening, and they both continued helping Kate host Jack's party. After a rousing game of Quidditch played in the backyard, the party began to break up. At last, just Lily and her family remained to clean up.

"I'm glad your birthday is on such a memorable day, Jack." Kate grinned as she washed dishes.

Jack looked up from sweeping the floor and grinned. "I might have read *Harry Potter* sooner if I knew what kind of party you would throw me just for agreeing to that theme."

Kate laughed, and Lily exchanged a grin with Will. They both knew Kate loved to throw themed parties, but normally Jack would rather eat birthday cake on the couch while watching a movie than participate in them. The party tonight had been fun for both of them.

"Speaking of things English, Princess," Jack began but was interrupted as a dishrag came flying at his face. Kate placed her hands on her hips while Will and Lily laughed.

"Would you stop calling me that!" Kate tried to keep an upset face but soon chuckled as Jack bowed to her.

"Your wish is my command," Jack intoned. "But seriously, guys, I have some news."

The laughter faded as they all looked at Jack. Lily noticed that he seemed rather nervous and wondered what would be causing that. Jack rarely felt nervous. She paused in her wiping down of the table to give him her full attention.

"Mom and Dad already know, but I got accepted into the University of Edinburgh. I start my master's classes this fall."

Stunned silence greeted his announcement, and Lily looked around in shock. She had no idea that Jack wanted to go back to the UK to continue his education. According to the looks on the faces of Will and Kate, they hadn't known either.

Lily spoke up first. "That's great, Jack! Congratulations! I had no idea you wanted to go there. When did this happen?"

"Well, I applied in October of last year while I was over there on my study abroad. I fell in love with Europe, the UK especially. You guys know my major was in archaeology and anthropology. I looked into it, and they have a master's in European archaeology. It seemed like a perfect fit."

"Forgive me for sounding like a downer," Will began, "but isn't that crazy expensive?"

"Yes, but I applied for some scholarships when I found out I was accepted. I just heard last month that I got one. School and some living expenses will be pretty well covered."

"You've known for a month?" Lily asked, surprised. It wasn't like Jack to keep secrets.

"Yeah." Jack looked a little embarrassed. "I wanted to make sure everything would work out before I told anyone. It wasn't an easy decision to make. But I'm excited to go, and I look forward to all of your visits."

Lily laughed along with Will and Kate. Trust Jack to get them to promise to visit before he'd even left. Lily knew she would love going. Jack shared her love of history, and she would enjoy seeing historical sites through his point of view, especially as he learned more in his studies. "Count me in," she said as she crossed to Jack and gave him a hug. "I'm so excited for you."

Will and Kate added their well wishes for Jack's new adventure. Lily thought that Jack's decision to go back to Scotland would give her an adventure of her own to look forward to. She couldn't wait to go visit him.

24
chapter

Lasting happiness is elusive, Lily reflected as she pushed her pen around on the desk at work. She had felt a little more like herself at Jack's party last week, but once again she felt emotionally numb. She supposed that pulling out of a depression as deep as hers required more than a temporary distraction.

Her shift tonight as the triage nurse was dragging, which wasn't helping. Women often came to the labor unit with various complaints. Some thought they were in labor, others were having early labor symptoms, and some came, Lily thought, because they didn't have anything else to do. The triage nurse was usually the first one to see them and help the doctors decide if the patient needed to stay and be treated or go home.

Usually, she liked helping the women who came to her unit, even the ones with non-labor related complaints, and the constant busyness of triage made the time go by quickly. Tonight, however, she felt like the shift was dragging on and on. It was barely past midnight, and though she'd sent home many patients from triage, she knew there was plenty of time for more people to walk through the door.

Kate's words kept echoing through her head as she continued pushing around her pen. What did she mean when she asked if Lily had forgotten who she was? She supposed that if she was being perfectly honest with herself, she knew that she had allowed some of her self-worth to be swallowed up in how Ammon felt about her. On the days she'd felt like he wanted to be with her, she was happy with who she was.

On those days when she felt him keeping his distance, however, she couldn't help but wonder what was wrong with her. She knew deep down that she had lots of things going for her, but she couldn't stop comparing herself with this Laura person. Somehow, even though she knew Laura wasn't a part of Ammon's life anymore, she couldn't help but feel like she didn't measure up. For some reason, Laura had a hold on his heart, and Lily felt like she would never break through. Now he was gone, and she would always feel like she had come in second place.

"Lil? You want to go get some lunch?"

Lily broke out of her reverie and looked over at Sara, the charge nurse, and realized that Trixie stood there as well. Trix must have finished transferring her patient to post-partum.

"I thought I'd send you and Trixie right now since we don't have any patients waiting to be seen," Sara continued.

"Works for me," Lily answered as she pulled herself out of her chair. She started walking with Trixie back to the break room. They both brought their lunches instead of buying them from the cafeteria. At this time of night, the options were limited and neither of them cared to spend lots of money on sub-par food.

"How're you doing?" Trixie asked as they sat down with their meals.

Trixie had been an amazing friend when Lily finally confessed everything that had happened when Ammon left. Minus her continued desire to egg his apartment, Trixie didn't say much about Ammon. She had tried to focus solely on Lily, which Lily was grateful for. Too many people had only negative things to say about Ammon and less patience to hear how Lily herself felt about the situation.

"I thought I'd be doing better by now," Lily answered truthfully as she picked at her sandwich. "At Jack's party last weekend, I felt more like myself, but now I'm back to just feeling numb inside. What's wrong with me? Why can't I just get over this and move on?" Frustration laced her words, and Lily was glad Trixie wouldn't take offense at her tone. Sometimes, she was tired of feeling so low, but she couldn't seem to figure out how to shake off the continual melancholy. There must really be something wrong with her.

"Lil, I'm about to ask a difficult question. I've been avoiding asking you for a while now, but I think it's time. Don't hate me, okay?" Trixie looked at Lily, as if asking for permission to go ahead with her comment.

Lily's eyebrows creased, but she nodded okay. Trixie took a deep breath before continuing. "Why is your self-worth wrapped up solely in how men feel about you?"

"What?" Lily looked surprised.

"Lil, you and I both know that you are an amazing person. You're educated, you're smart, you're driven to succeed, and you're talented in so many aspects of your life. You're kind, sympathetic, a great friend, and a loyal sister. Why do you choose only to focus on the fact that you're single to define who you are and how you feel about yourself?"

Lily sat back in shock; her lunch forgotten. She didn't do that, did she?

"When we were climbing a few weeks ago, what were you thinking about?"

"Um, well—"

"I know you were thinking about Ammon. It was written all over your face. And there's nothing wrong with remembering something good that happened with him. But you were thinking of the past and wishing that you could go back in time and relive that night all over again, weren't you?"

"Maybe," Lily answered defensively. "What's wrong with that?"

"What's wrong is that you can only see the person you were with him. You've forgotten that you, just you, are also someone of worth. He's gone, Lily, but you're still here. And *you* are worth loving. I want to be around you because I love you. Not because someone else thinks you're worth being around, but because you are one of my best friends and I couldn't imagine life without your friendship. You don't give yourself enough credit, Lil. Ammon left because of his own issues, not because you weren't enough."

At her words, Lily started tearing up. She held them in because she didn't want to cry at work, but she knew Trixie wouldn't lie to her. She wanted to believe her words so badly. She wished more than anything that she could feel like she was enough.

"I know it's going to take a while before you believe me," Trixie said, reading Lily's mind, "but I'm going to be here reminding you that you are enough. You've always been enough. The only person who truly can't see that is you."

Lily gave Trixie a wobbly smile and then quickly tried to compose herself as two other coworkers walked into the break room. She put on a fake smile and tried to keep up with the small talk floating around the table, but inside she kept pondering Trixie's words. She was enough. She wanted to believe it, and she hoped one day she would.

25
chapter

As with everything, Lily discovered, thoughts take time to change. Ammon had been in her life for about seven months, and yet the impact of his presence on her psyche was so strong, Lily felt like it would take a lifetime to move on. She'd never felt for anyone the way she felt for him and his loss had sent her spiraling into depression, but now she felt like she was finally beginning to see some light in her life again. Since her talk with Trixie in August, she'd tried to see herself the way Kate and Trixie saw her. Some days, she truly believed that she was a worthwhile person. Other times, she fell back into the familiar pattern of self-doubt and misery.

Kate and Trixie both continued to aid her in their own ways. Kate encouraged her to get out and be social again, even if it was just with family. It helped to have a safe place to go, where she wouldn't feel out of place. Dinners with Will and Kate became a weekly haven of comfort. Even when she didn't feel good about herself, she could always count on them to lift her mood with stories of their own antics. She appreciated their willingness to be with her no matter her frame of mind.

Trixie helped her find joy in exploring the outdoors again. Lily had always loved getting out into nature to hike and find solace in the beauty around her. Trixie organized a hike for them every week, and they were able to explore the seven peaks of Utah County, along with several other trails through the Wasatch Range. They even ventured north into Salt Lake County and found a few hikes in the canyons there.

Lily's favorite thus far was a hike that started at Brighton ski resort. The trail wandered past three different lakes: Mary, Martha, and Catherine. It then continued until it ran across the ridge of the mountains and connected in with the Great Western Trail, which runs from Canada to Mexico. She didn't have any aspirations to hike the entire thing herself, but she enjoyed connecting into it on her hikes and thinking about the many other feet that had come that way before.

She had hiked that trail with Trixie a few weeks before Jack left for Scotland. She had enjoyed it so much that she had managed to convince him to come with her and hike it again a couple of days before his departure. He had loved the views, and she treasured the pictures she took with him along the trail and at the summit. A picture of the two of them was now her phone's screensaver, and she loved looking at it and remembering the fun they had.

The memory associated with that picture still made her smile. She and Jack were nearing Lake Catherine, the last lake before they would take the short but steep hike up to the summit. Jack was telling her all about the classes he had signed up for as they rounded a bend in the trail. Jack stopped suddenly, and Lily looked up to see the largest bull moose she had ever seen standing mere yards off the trail.

They both froze for a moment looking at him. He looked back but just continued eating the foliage. Jack's large eyes caught hers, and she acknowledged his silent urging to back slowly down the trail. Once they made it back around the bend, Jack let out a huge sigh of relief, and Lily leaned back against a tree with a slight chuckle.

"Well, that's a new one," Jack said after a few minutes.

"I don't think I've ever run into a moose that close to the trail," Lily agreed. "How long do you think he'll stay there?"

Jack frowned in thought. "I don't know. Maybe we can look it up online. Moose feeding habits or something."

Lily laughed. "Jack, you think the answer to everything is online."

"Well, it usually is." He smiled as he pulled out his phone.

Lily grinned back as Jack began searching the Internet for ideas on what to do during a moose encounter. Jack never missed an opportunity to learn, no matter what the subject. Somehow, he always remembered the random things he looked up too, and Lily envied his memory.

"This article says that they'll usually move on after twenty minutes or so," Jack read.

"I guess we can wait him out then, if you're not in too much of a hurry."

"I can wait. Besides, the view from this spot is pretty amazing."

Lily agreed, and they spent their time waiting taking pictures of each other in random poses and talking about the adventures Jack had planned for when he was back in Europe.

Eventually, they peeked around the corner and realized the moose had moved on. They slowly crept past where he'd been, just in case he was still lingering unseen in the tall bushes. After a few minutes they'd finally started to relax, when all of a sudden there was a commotion just off the trail to their left. They had startled another bull moose, and they looked in time to see him bounding away farther into the trees. Jack missed a step and skidded to a halt, while Lily's hand flew to her chest.

After the moose was lost to the forest, Lily turned to Jack. They both looked at each other for a minute in shock, and then Lily started giggling as her nervousness ebbed into relief. Jack let out a loud laugh and shook his head. They'd laughed the rest of the way up the trail. It was a memorable hike to say the least.

She missed Jack, but she knew that he was enjoying his studies. It was October now, so he had been in Scotland for about two months. He didn't call often, but they were able to Skype and e-mail, and Lily loved hearing about all the new places he'd discovered.

On the days she felt more like herself, Lily dreamed of traveling back to Scotland again. She had loved her first visit there but hadn't been able to see as much of the country as she would have liked. Perhaps, if Jack made a few friends that happened to be girls, Lily could sleep on their couch and have a home base for her adventures.

Thinking of the future lifted her spirits for a time, but she also felt a deep sadness because she wanted so much to have these adventures with Ammon. No matter how hard she tried to put him firmly in her past, she still thought about him with every activity she did. She supposed it was inevitable that she would think of him, however, because they'd done so many things together.

Every time his memory surfaced, Lily tried hard to remember what Kate and Trixie had told her. As much as she loved Ammon, she knew she couldn't define herself by his actions any longer. She was finally starting to learn how to distance her feelings of worth from her feelings of missing him. The pain of his loss was still there, but ever so slowly it seemed she was realizing that she really did have value outside of her relationship with him. As wonderful as it once felt to be wanted by him, she knew she needed to learn to love herself before she would ever feel complete.

26
chapter

November came and the fall weather was quickly turning back into winter. Lily spent time in her kitchen every day making her favorite fall treats while the season lasted. As she slowly learned to appreciate herself for who she was, her enjoyment of her hobbies returned. Her coworkers seemed especially pleased by her return to baking.

In fact, in the midst of her lowest time over the summer, one of her coworkers had asked if she was okay. Surprised, because she always tried to hide her true feelings at work, Lily responded that she was fine. The coworker nodded in relief and then said that she'd been worried because Lily hadn't been bringing as many baked goods to work. Lily remembered laughing out loud at that comment. It was one of the first times she had laughed in months, and the mirth felt good even if it didn't last long.

Now Lily smiled as she prepared her goodies for work tonight. She had created caramel apple walnut cinnamon rolls with caramel cream cheese frosting. They were a masterpiece, if she did say so herself, and she was excited to share them. Especially because Trixie was working tonight, and Trix had a sweet tooth that would not be denied. After everything Trixie had done to help her start living life again, Lily felt like the least she could do was appease her taste buds.

After putting the finishing touches on the rolls, Lily hurriedly gathered her things. A small snowstorm was lazily dropping snow-flakes to the ground, and Lily didn't want to get caught up in the traffic the storms always seemed to create. For the first time in months, she felt happy just to be going to work. Perhaps, finally, she was starting to find herself again.

*****

Storms tend to bring in patients, and this night was no exception. Lily was glad she'd brought the cinnamon rolls; they were the only food she'd been able to eat all night. No one had time for lunch, and the patients just kept coming through the door.

Finally, at five in the morning, things started to settle down. Trixie was the triage nurse tonight and was sitting by the charge nurse, Sara, as Lily walked up to the main desk. Lily's patient had delivered and was now on post-partum, and she could see that Trixie had just finished sending someone home.

"I hate to ask," Lily said, "but are we finally caught up?"

"Yup, finally," Trixie responded with a sigh. "That was insane, even for us. Sometimes I don't even know how there are this many pregnant people in our area. I think I saw every single one of them tonight."

Lily laughed at Trixie's comment but knew how she felt. Some nights were pure crazy. She was about to respond to Trixie when, all of a sudden, she heard a code blue labor and delivery called on the intercom overhead. She looked in alarm at the speaker on the wall for a minute as it continued to emit information.

"Code blue labor and delivery, OR three," it repeated, and Lily's alarm changed to confusion. "We don't have anyone in OR three, do we?" she asked.

"Not as far as I know," Sara replied. "Would you and Trixie go back there and check it out? I'm going to call the operator to see who called the code blue."

Lily and Trixie hurried back to operating room number three. Lily was glad to already be in hospital scrubs. It saved time in situations like these where she was trying to be quick but still had to follow OR attire procedure. She and Trixie quickly donned their hats, masks, and shoe covers and rushed into the OR.

"It's empty," Lily said, stating the obvious while looking around. The lights were dim, and there wasn't a soul back there besides herself and Trixie.

"Well, I'm confused," Trixie added. "Do you think they meant to call it to the main OR?"

Lily turned toward Trixie but was distracted by a new voice saying, "Do you guys know what the code blue is about?"

Lily looked toward the wall of the OR and saw the neonatal nurse, Lisa, standing there on the other side of the pass-through window. This particular OR butted up to the neonatal intensive care unit, and the window enabled severely compromised babies to be passed directly into the NICU after they were born. It was a literal lifesaver.

"I have no idea," Lily responded. She opened her mouth to elaborate on their theory, when the doors to the OR opened behind her. She turned, expecting to see Sara coming to explain the situation. Instead, she felt her adrenaline start to race as a bed came flying into the room with two nurses pushing it, a doctor racing in behind them, and another nurse on top of the bed with the patient. A shared glance with Trixie, and Lily knew they had found their emergency.

"What's going on?" Lily heard Trixie ask the nurse on the bed as she rushed to get the bed into position to transfer the patient to the operating table.

"Cord prolapse."

Lily grimaced as she adjusted her mind to this new information. A cord prolapse was a true emergency, because if they didn't act quickly and perform a cesarean section now, the baby could die inside the mother from lack of oxygen.

"Her water broke at thirty-three weeks, and she's been in the hospital on the antepartum unit for the last few days. Everything was fine until she got up to go to the bathroom a few minutes ago. She said she felt a gush and then something coming out. When I went in to check, I saw the cord coming out. I'm elevating the baby's head off the cord, and luckily Dr. Jones was just outside the room when it happened."

Lily looked over to see the NICU personnel adjusting to the new information of a preterm baby about to be born. She knew they would have everything ready on their side when this baby came out. She returned her focus to her own tasks.

She had worked with Trixie long enough that they knew each other's rhythms. Trixie was gathering information from the patient's nurse as they worked quickly to prepare the patient for surgery. One of their OR scrub techs had followed the bed into the room and was preparing the instruments and other tools required to perform the surgery. Lily made the calls that would round up the other necessary staff to help with the emergency and then quickly began jotting notes for a timeline to help with charting later.

Sara followed the anesthesiologist and resident into the OR a moment later. She helped finish the final preparations for surgery, while Lily quickly performed the surgical count with the scrub tech.

Usually with cesarean sections, the anesthesiologist places a spinal block, which numbs the patient from the upper torso down but enables them to breathe on their own and stay awake during the birthing procedure. However, due to the emergent nature of this situation, there was no time to place a spinal block before surgery. The anesthesiologist quickly put the patient to sleep, and Dr. Jones and the resident moved rapidly to get the baby out and into the hands of the waiting NICU staff. A moment later, the baby emerged, and Trixie—attired to preserve the sterile field—gently took the baby from Dr. Jones and handed him through the window to the NICU team.

Lily glanced at the clock to note the time of delivery. Only fifteen minutes had passed since they first heard the strange code blue called overhead. Lily took a deep breath in amazement and glanced over at Trixie. Their silent look shared feelings of relief and awe. It never ceased to amaze Lily how quickly their team could move when faced with an emergency.

After a moment, Lily turned back to her tasks. The thought struck her that she had been essential in helping this delivery to happen, and she felt happy to have been a part of something so important. She began to smile softly as she recognized that there was worth to be found in her life after all.

27
chapter

The flames in her fire pit jumped and danced as Lily watched the fire gradually consume the stacked pine logs. Though it was cold this late in the evening, Lily stayed warm by cuddling into her bean bag chair and wrapping herself in a thick blanket. She'd dragged the chair into her backyard for her personal bonfire night celebration and congratulated herself on the coziness of her seat.

One of Lily's favorite British holidays was Guy Fawkes Day. Held on November 5 every year, it commemorated the arrest of Guy Fawkes back in 1605. He had been a part of the Gunpowder Plot group, which had been trying to blow up the British Parliament and the King by placing explosives under the House of Lords. The assassination attempt failed, and to celebrate the survival of King James I, people lit bonfires around London. The holiday gradually morphed into the present tradition of burning effigies, called "Guys," in huge bonfires, while watching firework displays and feasting.

Though the holiday didn't survive long in America after the pilgrims crossed the Atlantic, Lily still enjoyed lighting her own fire every year. She also decided this year to do something a little different. Instead of burning an effigy, she would instead write her feelings of loss and sadness down and throw them in the fire. She hoped that she could let go of some of her despair as she watched the embers burn.

She had felt inspired by a song she'd recently heard by Jordin Sparks called "No Air." The lyrics had hit her like a ton of bricks. The song described a woman and a man expressing their feelings about losing each other. It went back and forth between the two perspectives, and Lily felt that it perfectly described her relationship with Ammon.

She felt a new admiration for lyricists after her own attempts to write down her feelings. She wasn't even trying to write a song, but it was harder than she imagined to come up with just the right words to truly express her emotions. After several attempts and days of effort, she had finally come up with a short letter that she felt adequately portrayed her thoughts. Staring into the flames, she slowly reached her hand into her pocket and withdrew the folded sheet of paper. Opening it, she read the words one more time.

Dear Ammon,

I still love you. The days and months I spent with you are some of the best memories I have. Even as I write this, I can see your face as clearly as if you were sitting right next to me. Your smile and touch have invaded my dreams, and I hate waking up knowing that you're gone.

I wish that you'd never left. I wish I could understand why you felt the need to leave me behind instead of letting me support you in your battles. I hope you know that I would have fought with you, if only you would have let me.

I ache to hold you again, to tell you how much you mean to me. I miss the roughness of your hands as they gently held onto mine. I miss your strength, your kindness, your intelligence, and your light.

The pain of missing you takes my breath away. How am I supposed to move on when in my dreams we are still together? I wish it could be so. Wherever you are, whatever you are doing, I hope that you can feel my love for you. Even if

I can never say it again to your face, even if I find myself moving on, know that I'll forever hold you in my heart. I love you more than words can express.

Loving you forever,
Lily

She allowed the words to wash over her one more time. Her memories of Ammon were still so vivid, she felt like she could close her eyes briefly, open them, and he would be right there beside her. It was a fool's hope, and she thought back to the month after he'd left her. She'd felt so lost and confused that she'd written him and asked him to come back. In her message, she'd said she would take him as he was, no questions asked. All she wanted was to have him back in her life. When he'd finally responded weeks later, it was only to say that he wasn't coming back anytime soon. He had also said he felt like he was holding her back from progressing and that he couldn't hold onto her anymore. He'd told her she hadn't met the person she was meant to be with yet, and he didn't want to get in the way by being around.

Lily remembered reading those words. She'd been standing by her desk, and when she got to the end of his message, she fell to her knees sobbing. Any last remnants of hope for Ammon to return had fled, and she had felt completely bereft. That was the day that she had started falling into the bleak cavern of darkness that she'd lived in for so long. She couldn't imagine being happy again. She had felt sadness for herself, but even more so for Ammon. She knew that he was hurting, struggling to find worth in his own life, but he wouldn't let her be there for him. He'd pushed her away and convinced himself that it was for her own good. The months were long and dreary as the weight of her sorrow pressed down on her like a stone.

She'd seen some light in her life the last little while, however, and a small measure of hope had taken hold. As much as she still hurt for Ammon, she was starting to find reasons to live again instead of just exist. She looked once more at her fire dancing in the night and thought again about her dreams of a life with Ammon. She held them close to her heart for a moment, and then with a sigh she slipped her paper into the flames.

It caught fire rapidly and burned bright and hot for a brief moment. Then, all too quickly, the paper was consumed and the fire returned to the way it was before. Lily thought it was a good symbol of her relationship with Ammon. She just wished she could return to how she was before as easily as the fire could.

With a slight smile at her own melancholy thoughts, she took a deep breath and promised herself that she would work at moving on. She wouldn't forget her feelings for Ammon, but she would stop trying to live in the past. She closed her eyes to better enjoy the feel of the heat as the fire burned on.

*****

The Christmas season came and went. Lily had the holiday off this year, so she had traveled down to Arizona and spent time with her parents. Will and Kate had carpooled with her, and they had a great time singing Christmas songs at the top of their lungs all the way down. Jack stayed in Scotland since plane trips back were expensive, but they were able to have a video chat session with him to open presents and visit.

Lily loved being in Arizona for Christmas. While she enjoyed the snowy vistas of Utah, she adored being able to go out for walks in the warm evening weather to see the lights decorating the houses around her parents' neighborhood. She remembered that, as a child, she had always enjoyed using her outdoor Christmas gifts right away instead of having to wait until the spring. There were definite perks to a sunny Christmas season.

But the holidays were over now, and Lily had returned to her normal routine back home. She felt lifted after being with her family, though the clouds of depression still loomed. She continued to constantly question her own worth though Trixie, true to her word, continued to remind her of it every time she saw her.

In fact, Trixie had given her a small card for her birthday. "Open it in front of me before we leave the locker room," she remembered Trixie saying.

She'd worked the night before her birthday, and they were getting ready to start their shift. Usually Trixie wasn't so insistent about gifts, and Lily had wondered what in the world was in the small package in her hands.

"Trixie, what is this?" Lily asked, confusion furrowing her brow as she raised a small card up to read its message. The card read "I have worth."

"You're going to promise me right now that you will put it on your bathroom mirror and say the words three times every morning."

Lily had looked at Trixie questioningly and saw the seriousness of her gaze. "Okay, Trix. If it means that much to you, I'll do it."

"Good. And feel free to share the chocolates that I put in there too."

Lily laughed, and they did enjoy the chocolates throughout the night. She had remembered her promise to Trixie and placed the card in her bathroom when she got home. When she first started intoning the phrase each morning, she felt incredibly foolish. However, she kept repeating the mantra out of a sense of loyalty to Trixie. Soon, though, she felt like the words actually meant something to her. The more she looked at herself in the mirror and said those words, the more she believed they were true.

She pondered those words now as she walked through the neighborhoods near her home. When she woke up this afternoon, she had noticed that fresh new snow coated the world. She had decided to skip her run and go for a walk instead after shoveling her sidewalk.

It was twilight, and the world was quiet. Most people were still out of town enjoying time with family, so there were few cars on the streets. The snow hushed the normal sounds of busyness as people elected to stay indoors instead of venturing outside.

Lily loved the stillness the snow engendered. Walks had often been a source of solace in her life, and today, once again, the outdoors fit her mood perfectly. She felt introspective, and walking through the quiet of a snow-covered world helped her sort her thoughts.

Her memories of walks with Ammon lingered in her mind, but she pushed them aside today to make room for the feelings she had about herself.

The different questions asked by her family and friends over the past few months bounced around in her head. Had she forgotten who she was? Did she really feel like she had no worth just because she was single? She loved her time with Ammon, but would she allow his departure to continue to define how she felt about herself?

They weren't easy thoughts to dwell on. She'd never liked examining herself too closely, because she always felt like she didn't measure up to who she should be. But she was coming to realize that maybe she wasn't really being true to herself. Perhaps, she berated herself for her supposed failures more harshly than she deserved.

As she contemplated these new ideas, she came upon a house a few blocks from her home. Her lips lifted in an anticipatory smile as she looked up at the brown wood home. Eclectic would be a good description of its appearance. The plants hibernated now, but in the spring, Lily knew there would be flowers, shrubs, and trees filling and overflowing the small yard. The home itself looked cobbled together over the years, with additions headed this way and that across the small plot.

Lily's favorite feature, however, appeared on the eastern wall near where she now stood. A previous owner had used a small part of the brick chimney to carve a saying directly onto the house. She read again the familiar words, "Be pretty if you are, be witty if you can, but be kind if it kills you." She paused. She reread the words and focused on the last line: "Be kind if it kills you." She'd never given that line much thought. She always tried to be kind to everyone she met, no matter who they were. But this evening, for some reason, she finally thought about being kind to herself.

The tears, held in check so often over the last several months, began to flow, and there was nothing Lily could do to stop them. She was never kind to herself. She tried to accept compliments with grace but inwardly disagreed with the giver. She was the first to question her performance on anything from a piano piece to a batch of cookies. She never allowed herself to be human. In her mind, if she didn't do something perfectly, then she had failed. She gave everyone else the benefit of the doubt but refused to show herself the same compassion.

No wonder she could never find worth within herself. She held herself to impossible standards, and if anything went wrong, she figured it must be because she did not live up to who she thought she should be. No one is perfect, Lily knew, and yet she'd not given herself any slack over the years for being a normal human being.

These thoughts were an epiphany to her. All this time, she had blamed herself for Ammon leaving, for the fact that no man she encountered thus far had wanted to stay. She continuously defined herself by that perceived failing, but it wasn't all her fault after all. She had agency, and so did they. Whether or not a relationship worked out should not determine how she felt about herself.

These thoughts, perhaps obvious to many, felt so new to Lily. She was almost giddy at the release of pressure she experienced as they ran through her mind. The weight of all the past rejections in her life lifted as she focused on being kind to herself instead of blaming herself for others' choices.

It wasn't her fault Ammon left. She'd done everything she could to try and be there for him, to be a friend, and to be patient while he sorted out his feelings. Just because he decided not to pursue her didn't mean that she was worth any less. It had always been an option that he would stick to his desire of not wanting another permanent relationship. His decision had to do with his state of mind, not any lack on her part.

She had never felt angry at him for the choice he made, but now she understood even more clearly that she forgave him even as he broke her heart. It was herself that she had not forgiven. Now, however, she gave herself permission to be free from the weight of self-hatred she'd hung onto for so long.

Lily looked up at the night sky. The stars pierced the darkness of the moonlit night that had fallen as she'd stood next to the house, contemplating its message. The stars reminded her of one of her first outings with Ammon. She looked around until she found Orion. She silently sent Ammon a message of love and hope, of forgiveness and freedom. She hoped her thoughts would find their way into his heart through their shared celestial friend.

She knew she would always love him, but she allowed herself to be free of the thought that she had lost him. He had chosen to leave, and it was time to let the past be just a memory. Her future was as bright as her hope of good things to come.

28
chapter

Ammon looked through his camera one more time. It perched atop a tripod, ready to capture the stars moving through their orbits on this clear, cold January night. No moon interfered with the light, and he knew that his finished pictures would show streaks of starlight circling the North Pole as the world rotated through the night.

The camera position was perfect, so he began the long exposure that would secure the picture he wanted. He climbed up and then lied back on the hood of his car for a moment, looking at the stars. Though the location was different—he was currently in Wyoming instead of Utah—the thought of laying here next to Lily over a year ago caused his breath to hitch for a moment. He missed her. He knew he left her hurt and confused. After Laura showed up that fateful night, all he could think about was getting away. She'd come to ask him to take her back, but all he could think about was how she'd left him all those years before. She'd never even apologized for what had happened. She'd just assumed that he still missed her and that she could walk right back into his arms and pick up where they left off.

Ammon set her straight on that point very quickly. He had no desire to see, touch, or even associate with her again. He'd sent her out the door and on her way as quickly as he could. Even so, her appearance brought into force all his old feelings of pain and distrust. As much as he'd wanted Lily, as excited as he'd been for a future with her, his demons would not be silenced.

He'd walked to Lily's house a few days later, dreading what he needed to do with every footstep. Seeing her there in her yard nearly undid him, but he pushed his feelings aside. He wasn't good enough for Lily. He wasn't whole enough to make her happy, and he couldn't bear the thought of ruining the memories he had of their time together. So he'd said his goodbyes and then got as far away as possible before he could change his mind.

For several months prior to Laura's visit, his work had wanted to send him on an extended photography shoot to Asia. However, at the time they first mentioned it, he had stalled, not wanting to leave Lily for that long. But as soon as he had said goodbye to her, he'd sold his housing contract, packed up his bags, and headed out.

The months dragged by as his memories of Lily returned time and again with more and more force. He felt foolish for the way he had ended things, but he didn't know how to set it right. He was still fearful of fully committing to a relationship again, and the way he had responded to Lily's message a month after he'd left didn't leave him with many assurances that she would accept him back into her life, even as a friend.

If he was honest with himself, however, a friendship was not what he wanted. He still wanted Lily to be his, forever. It was the old inner debate: yearning for Lily but fearing what she would do when she figured out that he was not good enough for her.

He remembered a conversation he had with his mother a few weeks ago. She knew about his lingering feelings for Lily, even though he hadn't talked about her much for the last several months. A mother's intuition, he supposed. He had been home for Christmas and, not wanting to put a damper on the rest of his family's celebrations, he had tried to appear upbeat and happy. Still, he saw his mother watching him with a knowing look in her eye.

The night after Christmas he couldn't sleep, a common problem since leaving Lily. He had found himself staring into the last remaining embers of the fire smoldering in his parents' fireplace. He was remembering the night he spent with Lily, holding her while the flames danced in her wood burning stove and the inner fire he lit later when he instigated their first kiss.

Though the memory was pleasant, the emptiness of his arms only served to sharpen his longing for Lily. While he sat contemplating, he heard soft footsteps coming down the hallway toward him. It was nearly midnight, and he didn't think anyone else was still awake. He glanced up as his mother rounded the corner.

"Mom, are you all right?" he asked. Though he knew she'd always listened for him to come home before curfew during his teen years, his mother was naturally an early riser and liked to be in bed by nine. If she was awake now, then something must be wrong. Concern had him half rising out of his chair, but she quietly gestured for him to remain sitting. He settled back down into his recliner, and she took the matching one that sat next to his.

"Is a mother ever all right when her child is suffering?" she asked quietly a moment later. She turned to look at him, and the sadness in her eyes caught him by surprise. The depth of pain there seemed to reflect his own, and he quickly looked away.

"I'm fine, Mom," he said, looking into the fire once more.

"No, you're not, my son. I thought you were doing better several months ago, but it seems to me that you've slipped even farther away from the happiness you deserve but keep denying yourself."

Ammon's head lowered as her words hit home. Was it so obvious how much he missed Lily?

"Sweetheart, I know it's not my place to pry, but I'm worried about you. What happened?"

It wasn't like his mom to ask for details about his life that he hadn't openly shared. She believed in allowing him to make his own choices and deal with their consequences without needing to put in her two cents unless he specifically asked for her opinion. Her concern must truly be weighing on her if she felt the need to question him now.

He turned, intending to try and assuage her worry with some soothing platitudes, but the anguish on her face stopped him completely. Instead, he found himself unexpectedly yearning to confide in someone about his tangled-up emotions.

Haltingly, he described what had happened with Lily. His joy at being with her, his worry about not being enough, her willingness to bear with him while he figured out whether or not he could commit to someone again, and at last, Laura's fateful visit and the subsequent fallout. He left out how much he missed being with Lily physically. Though his feelings for her burned deep, that was a detail he was not comfortable talking about with his mother.

She listened patiently while he spoke, smiling when he described some of his dates with Lily and shaking her head in sadness at how he had ended things. Her eyes only narrowed briefly when he talked about Laura. His mother never spoke ill of anyone that he could remember, but she also never spoke about Laura at all.

After he finished telling her his story, he felt drained. He'd not allowed himself to truly feel the intensity of the emotions now pounding in his chest. For the first time since leaving Lily, he let the pain of his loss and failure take over, and he nearly drowned in the depths of it.

His mother continued to sit quietly, waiting for him to regain control of himself. After several minutes, he finally looked at her again. She reached out a hand, and he took it, finding comfort in the touch.

"Oh, my darling Ammon," she began, "I'm so sorry that you've had to go through such hard things. The pain of losing a loved one is something that never entirely goes away. I wish that this challenge hadn't come into your life. I wish that being with Lily was the easiest choice you ever had to make instead of the hardest. I can hear in your voice how much you miss her. I can see in your eyes the pain of her loss. But I'm going to tell you something now that will be hard to hear. I'm only saying it because I think that, in the long run, you will be happier for having considered my words."

She turned to grasp his hand firmly in both of hers, and her gaze seemed to penetrate his soul. "Son, you are making the biggest mistake of your life."

Ammon's eyebrows lifted in surprise, and his mouth reflexively opened to contradict her. Her small smile of understanding gave him pause once again, and she continued.

"I know you think that you must suffer in some way, do penance for whatever you think went wrong in your relationship with Laura. I have no idea why she made the choices she did, but those choices have taken her out of your life. Instead, you have the opportunity to be with this wonderful young woman. I've never met your Lily, but she sounds like she matches you better than anyone else you've ever dated. It is a rare person who would put her own feelings aside to give you the time you needed to be sure of your course.

"Now, I know you won't listen to me when I tell you how much worth you have. I'm your mother, so I'm biased." Ammon let out a small chuckle at this statement, but his mother ignored him and continued on. "But I can tell you this. You're intelligent, kind-hearted, talented, and, most importantly, worth loving. Your Lily seemed to think you had worth. Perhaps, you should trust her judgment more than your own in this case. You are worth loving, Ammon. I know that if you could feel that about yourself, you would have no problem committing to this patient and loving young lady."

She stood, though Ammon felt so shocked by her words that he barely registered her movement. She bent down and kissed him softly on his forehead like she'd often done when he was a child. "I'm going to leave you to ponder what I've said. I hope you know that I said it because I love you and want you to be happy. And I do love you so very much. Good night, son. I'll see you in the morning."

With that, she walked softly away, and Ammon was left alone to think. His mother was right in one respect for sure: leaving Lily was the biggest mistake he'd ever made. His thoughts turned back to Lily as he continued to stare into the fire. The rest of his mother's words were hard to cope with, and so he shoved them aside for the time being.

He managed to make it through the rest of his stay at home without dwelling too often on thoughts of his self-worth. Now that he was alone again, however, his mother's admonitions kept returning. He knew he had more to offer than he gave himself credit for. Admitting that, though, meant that he needed to act. He felt desperate to return to Lily, to see if she was willing to give him another chance, but fear of rejection and of still not being enough stopped him.

Ammon sighed and looked up at the stars. His eyes quickly found Orion. He wondered if Lily ever looked at the stars and thought of him. He always thought of her. He remembered what she'd said about Orion being her favorite constellation. Did she still tell him all her secrets, or had another man replaced both of them in her favor?

Thinking of Lily with another man still killed him inside. He loved her, but would he ever feel like he was the man that he needed to be for her? He wondered if he would ever feel whole enough to take a chance on a romantic attachment again. His thoughts continued to torture him with what could have been as the stars danced their slow circles in the heavens above.

29
chapter

Spring blossomed into new life all around her, and Lily felt the rebirth in herself that had been absent last year. Lily realized that she was slowly coming to see the value in loving who she was, not the unattainable epitome of perfection she thought she needed to be. It wasn't easy changing how she thought of herself, but time and good friends continued to help her realize her own worth.

Lily, the triage nurse again tonight, had no patients of her own for the moment, and so she ran around the hospital unit helping her fellow nurses get situated with the new patients that kept flooding the unit. The nurses all jokingly referred to spring as "lambing season," and the number of new babies being born bore testament to the renewal of life happening all around her.

Lily finished helping Trixie admit a patient, and they both walked out of the room to the nurses' station to take a breath. "This night is insane," Lily commented, plopping herself down in a chair.

"Agreed. Thank goodness there's only two more hours to go. My legs are aching from standing so much tonight," Trixie replied while taking a chair of her own.

"I hope they're not too sore to go climbing this afternoon."

"Not a chance. I've been looking forward to stretching my climbing muscles all week."

Lily smiled and then walked back to the front desk as Trixie started in on her charting. They had planned this climb a few weeks ago when they realized they both had the next few nights off. It would be a welcome respite from the busyness of the hospital.

Lily's good cheer about their afternoon adventure helped buoy her mood as she rounded the corner to the front desk and noted a fresh wave of women waiting to be seen. Never a dull moment tonight, it seemed. She took a deep breath and plunged into the next round of patients.

*****

"Oh, this feels so good," Lily exclaimed as she walked into the climbing gym later that afternoon with Trixie. Though it was mid-April, it was still cold to be climbing outside, so they'd both agreed to climb indoors.

Trixie laughed. "We haven't even started yet."

"True, but just knowing we get to go conquer some wonderfully difficult routes makes me feel really happy."

"I'm glad. In fact, I was going to mention this before, but I noticed that you seem a lot happier in general lately. What's changed?"

"Nothing and everything," Lily answered seriously. She took a look around the gym while they checked in, then continued her thought as they walked toward a vacant wall. "I finally decided to listen to what you and Kate have been telling me all along. I'm worth loving, and my life has meaning. It just took me a while to see that I hadn't been treating myself fairly at all. You were right when you said I defined myself by what I lacked. When Ammon left, I couldn't see the truth of the situation through my own pain and self-loathing. But now, it's different." Lily paused as she looked around the gym. She gestured toward a wall.

"Ammon and I climbed that wall together. Before, the only feeling I would get from that memory was a longing to be back in that time. I couldn't look forward because I wanted to live in the past. Now I can see that memory and be thankful for the joy it brought me. But I also realize that, if I want to move forward, I have to make new memories. I might not be ready to date again, but that doesn't mean I can't live my life the way I want to right now. I have friends and family who love me, and that's enough for the moment."

Trixie's smile had grown with each passing word, and now she wrapped Lily in a spontaneous hug. Lily felt the warmth of her embrace and allowed herself a moment to think of the progress she had made because of support from good friends like Trixie. She was so happy that Trixie was a part of her life.

"You just made my day," Trixie said after they ended their hug. "I've been worried about you, but there was never a great moment to bring it up at work. I wish our schedules had worked out better the last few months. I've missed hanging out with you."

"I agree. You always brighten my day. I hope this next schedule lets us have a few more days off at the same time so we can go on some more adventures," Lily responded as she fished out her gear and stepped into her harness. She started grabbing her shoes when she caught a glimpse of Trixie's face out of the corner of her eye. "Trix? What's wrong?"

"Oh, Lily. I don't know the best way to say this. I'm moving." Trixie looked away as she finished speaking.

"What do you mean you're moving? Up to Salt Lake or something? You know I'll drive up to see you."

"I wish it was going to be as close as that." Trixie hesitated. She took a deep breath and said, "I'm moving back east."

Lily stared at Trixie in shock. She had never said a word about wanting to move and especially not so far away. Why in the world did she want to leave?

Trixie must have seen the hurt beginning to form on Lily's face for she hurried to say, "I'm sorry I didn't say anything sooner, but the truth is that these plans just barely came about. I wasn't even thinking about going anywhere until just recently. But something happened that made me realize it was time for me to move on. I'm so sorry, Lily. I'm really going to miss you." Trixie looked so dejected that Lily decided to swallow her own hurt and simply focus on Trixie right now. "Where back east are you going?"

"I'm not sure." Trixie hedged, and Lily noticed that she looked even more uncomfortable now. Why didn't she want to tell Lily where she was going?

"Well, when you figure it out, will you let me know so I can come visit you?"

Trixie looked relieved. "I'd like that. I'm sorry I'm being so vague. There's a reason, but I really don't want to get into it right now. It's my fault it got to this point. I usually don't get too close to people so it's easier when I leave, but we got along so well, it was impossible not to become friends."

Lily felt a little blindsided by what Trixie just told her. She thought about it and realized that what Trixie said was true. She'd never really noticed, but Trixie did seem to have her as her only good friend at work. Oh, she was friendly enough with the other nurses and staff, but she never talked about doing anything with them outside of work. Lily couldn't remember Trixie telling them anything personal about her life either.

Come to think of it, how well did she really know Trixie? She knew they shared similar senses of humor, they enjoyed many of the same activities, and Trixie was the one person she felt comfortable opening up to about her own struggles. But in all the time they'd been friends, she had never really found out much about Trixie's past. Was her past the reason why she felt she had to leave? What had happened to her?

Lily's thoughts were running through possible scenarios, and she unintentionally blurted out, "Are you in witness protection or something?"

Trixie let out a little laugh, and Lily could sense some bitterness in it. "Not so much. It's a long story, Lil, and I'm not comfortable sharing it often. Suffice to say, I got myself into a situation that caused me a lot of grief. Sometimes I just need to change where I am to let the past stay in the past."

Lily couldn't argue with that. She had spent a whole year trying to overcome her own memories of the past. If moving could help Trixie with that, then she wouldn't try and stop her. "When are you leaving? Have you already given your two weeks?"

"I gave it last week. I'm moving in two days. Last night was actually my last shift at work."

"What? But we didn't have a going-away party or anything for you!"

"I didn't want to make a big fuss about it. No one will even miss me except for you."

Lily felt saddened by the fact that Trixie was leaving so abruptly, though she could understand her desire to keep her personal life to herself. But she would miss working with her and spending time having different adventures together.

"Just make sure you move near a place where we can climb," Lily finally replied as she reached down to grab her shoes. "I'd hate to come for a visit and not be able to enjoy one of our favorite activities."

"Done," Trixie replied, reaching now for her own gear. She looked as if a weight had lifted off her shoulders, and Lily felt glad Trixie trusted her enough to share part of her own story. It didn't stop her from being curious about the details of Trixie's prior life though. Perhaps, in time, she would learn the whole truth behind Trixie's shadowy past.

30
chapter

Lily spent the next day at Trixie's apartment helping her pack and clean. She had visited before, but it dawned on her as she moved boxes to the car just how few things Trixie possessed. Another sign of a life lived without permanence.

Lily had come back this morning to wish Trixie farewell and to help carry the last few essentials out to the car. "Even though you don't have that many things, I still didn't think we'd get them all to fit in here," Lily said as they put the last box in the back and closed the trunk.

"Oh, she's got lots of room," Trixie replied, lovingly patting her car. "We've traveled a lot, and I've never had any problems. She's a keeper."

"If only men could be as reliable as your car," Lily quipped.

They both shared a laugh, but it didn't last long. Lily dug sadly into her purse and handed Trixie an envelope.

"What's this?"

"I don't know where you'll end up or what amazing culinary options will be there. But when you do settle in, I want you to enjoy some local cuisine on me. Just make sure and tell me all about it."

Trixie peeked in the envelope and saw the stack of bills Lily had stuffed inside. Lily had never seen Trixie cry before, but she noticed now that her eyes glistened. Lily fought back her own tears.

"I've got something for you too," Trixie said, pulling a small bag from the dash of her car and handing it to Lily. Lily opened it and reached inside. The bag contained a necklace with a small crescent moon and a star floating on the strand. "It's so you remember that

I love you to the moon and back, and I want you to reach for the stars."

The threatened tears began to steal down Lily's cheeks. She would miss her friend so much. They wordlessly moved to give each other a hug. Too soon, they broke apart and Trixie got into her car. Lily watched from the sidewalk as Trixie slowly pulled out of the parking lot and onto the road.

With a sigh, Lily began walking toward her own car. Though Trixie's departure didn't hurt as much as Ammon's, Lily decided she was tired of being the one left behind. Perhaps it was time to consider a new adventure of her own.

*****

Later that evening, Lily made her way over to Will and Kate's for their weekly dinner. She kept thinking about her desire for a new adventure. Maybe Kate would have some ideas for her.

"Lily!" Kate exclaimed as she opened the door and ushered her inside. "You'll never guess what happened."

Lily hadn't seen Kate looking this excited for a while. It had to be something big. "Tell me!"

"Jack's got a girlfriend."

Lily looked stunned. She talked with Jack all the time, but he'd never said anything about a girlfriend. In fact, Jack was friends with everyone, but never before had he singled out a girl to date. He focused so much on his studies that their whole family wondered if he would ever get his nose out of a book long enough to notice anyone.

"Tell me about her," Lily replied, sitting down on the couch in Kate's living room. She sank into its microfiber softness and felt Kate's excitement start to stir her own.

"Now, wait just a minute," Will's voice interrupted from the kitchen. He came around the corner in an apron and holding a stirring spoon.

Lily began laughing at his appearance, and Will looked at her to see what was so funny. When he saw her eyes trained on his apron, he gave an affronted look and said, "I don't want flour all over my good lounge wear."

This only made Lily laugh harder. Will didn't own a manly apron of his own, so he had borrowed one from Kate. The white fabric was edged with Christmas colored frills, and the front displayed a gingerbread man decorated for the holidays. The caption on the front said, "All I want for Christmas is a man made of dough."

"Keep that up and you won't get any of my monster cookies," Will replied, shaking the stirring spoon threateningly in Lily's direction. She managed to stifle her laughter but couldn't entirely stop the mirth from sneaking out in a few more small giggles.

"Anyway," Will said, dramatically, "Jack doesn't have a girl-friend. He has a girl that is a friend."

"You weren't reading between the lines," Kate interrupted. "He talked about her more than he's ever talked about another woman."

"Mentioning her three times in the course of an hour-long conversation doesn't mean he likes her like that," Will answered back, placing his hands on his hips.

Lily's giggles threatened to burst out again. Will's gruff determination to defend Jack against spurious accusations of love contrasted perfectly with the little cartoon gingerbread man dancing across his chest. Before she could think through her words, Lily said, "Why don't I just travel to Scotland and assess the situation in person?"

Will and Kate both ceased talking and looked at her. Kate looked thoughtful for a moment and then said, "I think that's an excellent idea."

"Lily can't just go to Scotland on her own," Will interjected.

"Will, I'm thirty years old, and it's Scotland. It's not like I'm trying to go to the Middle East alone. I speak the language, I've been there before, and Jack will be there this time too. I'll be fine. In fact," Lily began feeling more excitement as her thoughts fell into place, "I've been feeling like I need to get away on an adventure anyway. This is perfect. I can look into the Jack situation, and I can go to all the sites I didn't get to see on my first trip across the pond."

"I think it'll be great for you to take a vacation," Kate agreed. "You've only been traveling a little this last year, and you haven't taken any big trips for a while. Plus, I'm really interested in your take on Jack's girlfriend."

"His friend that's a girl," Will added. "Well, as long as you're careful, I guess it's okay."

"Thanks, Dad," Lily teased.

"Hey, I'm just trying to watch out for you. You never know what you're going to run into when you travel."

"Hopefully a hot Scottish man that sweeps her off her feet," Kate remarked.

Lily laughed as Will looked shocked. "What do you mean a hot Scottish man? Is all this not hot enough for you?" He gestured to his apron-covered figure, and Kate joined Lily in her laughter. Will looked down and remembered he was still wearing the apron. He let out a little laugh, shook his head, and walked back into the kitchen. "I have cookies to finish," they heard him say as he disappeared around the corner.

"Seriously, Lil," Kate continued once their laughter had subsided, "keep your eyes open. You never know who you might meet."

Lily grinned. She didn't know what this trip had in store for her, but she felt like something wonderful was headed her way.

31
chapter

Of course, as much as Lily wanted to hop on the next flight to Edinburgh, she had to wait a few months for it to fit into her schedule at work. She finally arranged her time off for August. She hadn't used any vacation hours in years, so she took three weeks off. She hoped she could see all the places she wanted to in that time. To that end, she spent the months leading up to her trip immersed in literature about Scotland. She researched the best places to see, favorite locations off the beaten path, inns, restaurants, transportation, and local events.

She fell into a familiar pattern as the summer months moved along. On her days off, she woke up in the early afternoon to go for a run up the canyon or hike a new trail. In the evenings, she would do her research. Gradually, she formed a plan of the places she most wanted to see and the ways she would travel through the country to get around.

She had decided she wanted to rent a car. She preferred traveling on her own timetable and not being constrained by tour groups or local transportation times. She started visualizing driving on the left side of the road. Even when she crossed streets, she consciously tried to imagine looking at cars coming from the opposite way to prepare herself for her pedestrian touring days.

It was now the end of July, and her vacation was just over a week away. Lily had contacted Jack when she first started planning her trip, and he had arranged to have her stay with some friends from the university. She was glad one of them was the girlfriend they'd continued to hear about. Lily felt eager to meet her.

She thought about Jack and his girlfriend now as she walked along her chosen path for the day. The trail followed the Provo River, which flowed from the mountains and down into the valley. She'd started at Nunn's Park and slowly made her way up the trail, past several waterfalls, and into a more forested area of the path.

She'd begun her walk in the early evening to avoid the heat of the day. Besides the mosquitoes, the path was deserted. It helped that it was a Tuesday night, and it seemed that most people were home for dinner. Many of them were probably dining as families, Lily thought with a sigh. Learning to love who she was hadn't stopped the longing for a permanent male companion in her life. She looked around at the trees and thought about the last time she had walked this trail. Ammon had brought her here that first fall when they were just friends, before things had become complicated.

She remembered how she'd felt then. She couldn't believe her luck to be walking beside this man she admired. How smart and capable he had seemed as he explained the different types of trees and foliage as they had walked past.

He was strong too. He had lifted her up enough to pull herself up on a branch of a tree they had decided to climb. She couldn't quite reach it, and he had hoisted her with ease and then made the jump himself onto the same limb. She smiled now remembering her laughter as they made their way up the branches like giddy little children. Then they had sat, perched high in the air, for quite some time as they talked about different experiences from their childhoods.

Lily sighed as the memory washed over her. Thinking of Ammon no longer depressed her, but she still felt sad that he had chosen to leave. The woman she was when she climbed that tree had learned so much from the experience of having him in her life. But she had learned even more after he left.

She'd come to love who she was. Part of her wanted to show Ammon what he had inadvertently done for her. It was because of him that she had finally become the woman she wanted to be. She wished she could have the chance to thank him somehow for the trials that had only made her stronger in the end.

With a smile, she acknowledged that if she was being completely honest with herself, she wished Ammon would see the new her at a time when he was open to seriously dating again. She had never stopped hoping that he would change his mind about his self-enforced romantic isolation.

She took a deep breath and let the thought slip away into the twilight. She knew she had to move on. He wasn't coming back. The corners of her lips lifted as she thought about Scotland. Maybe Kate was right. Maybe a little Scottish fling was just the kind of therapy she needed right now.

32
chapter

Lily made a face and tried not to spit the contents of her mouth back into her cup. She gamely swallowed and then grimaced as the bubbly liquid hit her stomach. "That's disgusting," she finally announced when she got her gag reflex under control. "Why in the world would anyone drink that?"

The room erupted in laughter around her, and Lily joined in. Jack lightly punched her arm and said, "It's just seltzer water, Lil. Everyone drinks that around here."

"No wonder our ancestors migrated to America. That stuff should be outlawed."

Another round of chuckles, and the attention in the room gradually returned to the soccer, excuse her, football match currently playing on TV. Lily tucked her legs under her, placed her drink on the end table, and looked toward Jack. She sat on the small arm chair to the left of the loveseat where Jack sat with Brooklyn.

They were in Jack's apartment, which he shared with another master's student. The space was small, but Jack told her he wasn't here that often so it didn't really matter to him. He spent most of his time at the university working on his studies. He also spent a good chunk of time at Brooklyn's apartment. Lily turned her attention to the woman seated on Jack's right. Brooklyn was absolutely gorgeous. She had dark curly hair, smooth brown skin, and a figure to die for. Lily was also jealous of her soft English accent. It fit her beauty completely.

And yet Brooklyn was also one of the most down-to-earth people Lily had ever met. She seemed to give little attention to her outward appearance. She dressed casually and neatly but didn't use much makeup or other beauty-enhancing products. She didn't need them in Lily's opinion.

When she'd first arrived in Edinburgh two days ago, Lily had rented her car and drove to Brooklyn's apartment. Brooklyn had graciously agreed to give Lily full run of the couch whenever she needed it while she was in Scotland. Lily planned on taking several trips into the highlands and wouldn't always be in town, but it was nice to have a home base all the same.

Jack had arranged to meet her there the first time she arrived, and Lily eagerly anticipated her first introduction to Jack's girlfriend. When Brooklyn opened the door and invited Lily in, Lily could see why Jack would seek out Brooklyn's attention. Brooklyn had immediately made Lily feel welcomed and comfortable. Her apartment was clean and decorated to promote a feeling of relaxation. Lily loved it instantly and thought Brooklyn fit Jack's personality perfectly.

But then Lily started to be a little uncertain about what their relationship truly was. Brooklyn didn't act like Jack's girlfriend. They were friendly enough together, but she didn't see any intimate behavior from either of them. Granted she'd spent the first day touring several of the sites around Edinburgh and hadn't really been in their company much, still it seemed as though Will might be right. Brooklyn seemed more of a friend who happened to be a girl instead of a girlfriend. Kate would be disappointed.

"Hey, Lil," Jack's voice interrupted her train of thought, and she quickly focused on what he was saying. "I'm going into the kitchen to grab some more snacks. You want any?"

"Sure. Just bring me whatever you're having."

With a thumbs-up, Jack rose off the couch and moved into the kitchen. Now was her chance. "So, Brooklyn, how do you put up with my brother over there anyway? Hasn't he driven you crazy yet?"

Brooklyn looked over at Lily and smiled. "Not in the slightest," she replied easily. "We get on quite well, and it's nice to have an American friend again."

"Oh, that's right. Jack told me you spent some of your early years in the States."

"I did. My mother met my father when he was stationed at Lakenheath here in England. They fell in love, and she decided she would be okay living as the wife of an Air Force officer. So they got married, and when his assignment sent them back to the States, she went with him."

"I would have thought from your accent that you'd grown up in England your whole life."

Brooklyn smiled sadly. "I've been here since I was five. My father died when I was young, and my mother moved back to England to be closer to her family again."

"Oh, I'm so sorry to hear that. I had no idea."

Lily didn't ever remember hearing that story from Jack. Though, to be honest, he'd kept his comments about Brooklyn mostly superficial. He had mentioned the hobbies they had in common, but never much of her personal history.

"You didn't know, and it was a long time ago. I'm sorry I never got a chance to grow up with him, but my mum is amazing. Perhaps I'm partial, but I think she did rather well."

"That she did," Lily agreed with a laugh, noting Brooklyn's playful expression. She liked this girl more and more. "So I'm just curious. Are you dating anyone?"

Brooklyn looked a little uncomfortable at the question, and Lily wondered if she was on the right track. "You don't have to answer that. I know it's personal. I was just curious if there were any men around here worth checking out. I'd hate to start liking someone who was already taken."

"Oh, there's plenty of good men. Getting them to realize that there's more to life than studying and research might be difficult though."

Interesting. Lily decided to press just a little bit more. She looked toward the kitchen and noticed that Jack had started a conversation with another friend. From the way they were gesturing excitedly, she figured she had a few minutes before he came back over.

"Okay, I'm just going to ask. Jack's been talking with us, and by us I mean me, my brother Will, and his wife Kate, about what he does over here. Your name has come up several times, and so we're all curious. Is there something going on between the two of you?"

Brooklyn laughed a little and glanced toward Jack. Lily noticed, finally, a look of longing in her eyes before she turned her attention back to Lily.

"I wish I knew," Brooklyn admitted. "We've been friends since a few weeks after he got here, so almost a year now. At first, I thought he was going to ask to date me, but then school really picked up, and he's been buried in his books ever since. We'll do activities together on occasion, but it's never progressed past a friendship."

Lily shook her head at her brother's ignorance. "Jack might be extremely book-smart," Lily commented, "but when it comes to common sense there is definitely a disconnect."

Brooklyn laughed as Jack walked back over to the couch.

"What's so funny?" he asked, looking between the two of them.

"Oh, we were just talking about the rarity of common sense," Lily replied with a wink at Brooklyn. She took her plate of snacks from Jack and turned back toward the football match. Lily would keep her conversation with Brooklyn private, but she would definitely see if she could push Jack into opening his eyes while she was here. Brooklyn seemed like someone worth keeping.

33
chapter

Lily spent the next two days in Edinburgh, and she spent one full day just exploring the Royal Mile. Of course, much of that time was at Edinburgh Castle itself. She loved all medieval buildings, but castles were her favorite, and she tried to explore every single part of the old fortress. The views from the castle itself were amazing and prompted today's adventure of a hike up Arthur's Seat, an ancient extinct volcano near Edinburgh. The hike was not too difficult, the peak summiting at a mere 823 feet, but the views across Holyrood Park and into Edinburgh itself were well worth the climb.

Brooklyn joined her today, claiming she needed an excuse to leave her studies behind for the morning, and Lily happily agreed to her company. As they hiked, Lily took the time to learn more about Brooklyn. She discovered that Brooklyn had grown up in Newmarket, which was less than fifteen miles from Cambridge University. Brooklyn told her that it was trips to Cambridge as a young girl that had awakened her love of history, though her passion was focused on architecture instead of archaeology like Jack. She explained that Cambridge University had architectural styles ranging from the Anglo-Saxon period to more modern styles and that seeing the different types of buildings had fostered a desire in her to learn more about the people who built them.

"I have to admit," Lily said, "that whenever I think about Cambridge, I just picture Trinity College. I had no idea that there were so many other styles of architecture there too. Though, since it's been around so long, I guess it makes sense. I don't imagine modern architects would really want to construct new buildings in a Renaissance style."

Brooklyn laughed. "I don't suppose they would. Too bad, though, I rather like looking at that type of design. It's been awesome to be learning here in Edinburgh too. Besides the castle, there are so many older structures still in existence that are now mixed in with the newer buildings. I feel happy just walking down the streets and seeing the difference.

"Even though I was really sad when my father died and we moved back to England," she continued, "it's truly been a blessing for someone like me who likes looking at buildings from hundreds of years ago. I can cross the Channel and be in Paris in a matter of hours or go down to Wales and tour through the castles there. Ireland is full of beautiful ruins from ancient times. I'm afraid America doesn't quite have the same access that I have here."

"I'll give you that one," Lily agreed. "As much as I love the ancient Native American sites and the gorgeous natural vistas through the West, I would love to live here and have the ability to see this history so often and easily."

"You could always move here too." Brooklyn smiled.

"Tempting. Plus, then I could encourage Jack to stop studying so much and have a social life."

They both laughed at the thought and then turned their attention to the view as they reached the top of Arthur's Seat. They'd climbed the popular circular route to the top, enjoying the different views as they went. The occasional unpaved and somewhat steep and rocky sections of the climb made her rock-climbing heart happy, but the trail still hadn't been too difficult to transverse. The first part of their hike showcased views of Edinburgh's Old Town, while the portion crossing over Salisbury Crags had an amazing view of the castle. They zigzagged their way up to the summit from there.

The wind whipped at her as she looked out from the summit, and she could see heather and wild flowers stretching across the ground down the hillside. In the distance, she could see St Anthony's Chapel standing high on a rocky outcrop above St Margaret's Loch.

Edinburgh stretched out before her, and Lily felt a sense of awe thinking about the history that lived all around her.

"It's a beautiful view, isn't it?" Brooklyn asked after a few moments.

"Amazing. Totally worth the hike to get up here and see it. I can see the old buildings and monuments, the castle, the lochs, and even the sea. I'm hooked. I wonder if they'd let me build a house up here."

Brooklyn laughed, and Lily chuckled too, though deep down she wished there could be a way to live somewhere that had this view all the time.

After spending a good hour at the summit, they finally began the hike back to the car. They started exchanging different anecdotes about Jack while they descended from the peak. Lily couldn't help giggling at some of the situations Brooklyn had been in with him. "And no one found you two for over half an hour?" Lily laughed at the end of one of Brooklyn's stories.

"Nope. They looked in every single room except the one in which we hid. I couldn't believe it. And of course, we couldn't just leave until we were sure everyone else had been found. I still can't believe that we stuffed ourselves into a broom cupboard for that long."

Lily laughed again at the thought. Leave it to Jack to come up with a version of hide-and-seek that could be played as an adult. Apparently, he thought it was a great idea to hide in teams of two, thereby making it more difficult to find a suitable hiding spot. Lily laughed again at the idea of her 6'3" brother tucked inside a closet.

"Oh, man. I'm going to have to ask him about that one," Lily said as they reached the bottom of the hill. "That reminds me, I'm having dinner at Jack's tonight. He said you were invited too, if you want to come."

"I already have a study group planned, I'm afraid," Brooklyn answered, looking disappointed. "Another time though."

"Absolutely." If Lily had anything to say about it, Brooklyn would receive many more dinner offers from Jack in the near future. In fact, maybe this was the perfect time to open her baby brother's eyes to what he was missing.

*****

"Okay Lil, are you ready to try some real Scottish cuisine?" Jack asked, rubbing his hands together.

Lily, who had just walked in the front door, looked warily over toward Jack's kitchen. "And who, pray tell, cooked up this masterpiece?"

It was a well-known fact in their family that Jack's cooking was the worst. With as much as he loved to eat, Lily thought he would have improved over time, but he remained tragically unable to make anything more complicated than macaroni and cheese.

"It might have been the pub down the road, but at least it's hot." Jack laughed. He knew his own failings at cooking as well as anyone, and he didn't mind admitting his weakness. It was one of his more endearing characteristics. They sat at the table and fell on the food with relish.

"This is really good," Lily said, as she reached for another serving. "Remind me what this one is called again?"

"Neeps and tatties," Jack replied with a smile.

"The name needs work, but I can't argue with the flavor." Lily smiled.

"I skipped the haggis and just went with bangers as our main dish. What do you think?"

"I think you made a wise choice, bro. I applaud your meal-making decisions. But most importantly, what's for dessert?"

Jack chuckled and reached around for a paper bag. He knew Lily's sweet tooth would want to try more than just traditional dinner foods. "Tablet."

"That sounds like an electronic device, though I'm sure their dessert used the name first. What is it?" Lily reached inside the bag.

"Tablet is made up of sugar, condensed milk, and butter that cooks together until it's crystalized. It's delicious."

Lily didn't want to wait to finish her main meal before tasting dessert and quickly took a bite of the sweet treat. Her taste buds danced for joy as the sugary concoction hit her tongue. She closed her eyes to savor the flavor.

"I fully approve. You've convinced me. I'm moving to Scotland."

Jack laughed as he finished his meal and then took a piece of tablet for himself. He ate slowly, and when he was finished, he nodded in Lily's direction. "I think you could do well here, Lil. It fits your personality. This place is imbued with the echoes of time. History walks down the streets wherever you turn. Yes, I think you would like it very much."

"Very poetic, Jack. Have you ever tried using some of those lines on a fair maiden?" Jack turned a little pink, and Lily knew at once that he was holding something back. "Ah, so there is a lady you admire. Could it be the beautiful Brooklyn?"

Jack looked away, but Lily saw a small smile play across his lips. "She's a wonderful person and a really good friend. I'm glad you've had a chance to get to know her."

"Jack." Lily looked at him seriously. "Why aren't you dating her?"

Jack looked uncomfortable for a moment and then let out a sigh. "I don't know how to. I'm so busy with school, and I don't want the girl I date to feel like she comes in second place. I just feel like I can't devote my time to both things right now."

Lily nodded slowly in understanding. This was classic Jack. He always made sure that he put a lot of time and emphasis on the people in his life so as not to leave them thinking he didn't care about them. Lily could see that he worried about not being able to spend enough time with Brooklyn to make her feel important to him.

"Can't you tell her how you feel and then tell her the reasons why you've waited so long to be with her? I'm sure she'll understand. After all, she's a student too. Besides, you can't study all the time. You need to have a life outside of scholarly pursuits too."

"I know, Lil. But we've been friends for so long now, and she's never said anything. What if she's not interested in me? I don't want to make our friendship weird."

"Oh, Jack. That's just a chance you'll have to take. But if you want my completely partial opinion, I think you two would be great together, and I think she might think that too."

Jack looked cheered by Lily's comment, and Lily felt happy that she could at least try to help Jack and Brooklyn. She knew how hard uncertainty in relationships could be. If she could help them overcome this first hurdle, she would feel like she'd really made a difference during her time in Scotland.

34
chapter

Lily stood in the crowd and let the sound of bagpipes wash over her. She closed her eyes as the melody of "Scotland the Brave" sounded through the air. It had been a week since her dinner with Jack, and Lily now found herself at the Cowal Highland Gathering eagerly anticipating a few days of watching the Highland Games there. Everywhere she looked, she saw men in plaid kilts getting ready to participate in the heavy events taking place throughout the area. She couldn't wait to watch a caber toss and looked forward to seeing a real Maide-leisg, or, as she knew it, a game of stick pull.

She opened her eyes as the bagpipes finished. The first competition she wanted to watch today, though, was the beginning dances of the annual World Highland Dancing Championship. Lily loved Scottish dance; she had even taken a class once at school. Her feet were not nearly as nimble as the performers now taking the stage, however. She marveled at the strength of the performers' arms and legs. They looked so graceful as they stepped and turned. The sight made her wish she had kept up with the steps she'd learned in her class.

"Are you an admirer of the dance?" a low timbered voice sounded near Lily's ear.

With a small start, Lily looked to her left and found the body to whom the voice belonged. And what a body it was, she realized as she took in the whole sight of him. His hazel eyes danced as he looked at her, and she noticed that his shaggy brown hair seemed ready to take flight in the light breeze. His arms and legs were well muscled, and she realized she was noticing his legs because he was clothed in a traditional kilt, leaving his calves uncovered. The blue, green, and black-striped pattern of his kilt complimented his physique perfectly.

Lily realized she was staring open-mouthed at him and quickly pressed her lips together. "It's beautiful," she finally replied, still gazing at the stranger.

"It doesn't compare with you, lass," the stranger said. "I'm Liam Campbell." He held out his hand, and Lily took it with a smile.

"Campbell. An appropriately ferocious Scottish name."

"Ah, so you know some of the history of our fair land."

She gently took her hand from where it still rested in his, her heart beating as fast as the rhythm of the music. She was attracted to this man, she realized. It had been so long since she felt the sensation, she'd almost forgotten what it was like. She still didn't like those rambunctious butterflies. "I do indeed. Lily Manning."

His now empty hand covered his heart on his chest, and he sighed dramatically. "An English name and an American accent. The fates have cursed me to fall for a foreigner."

Lily laughed at his dramatics. "Don't be too fooled by the last name," she countered. "There's a fair amount of Scots blood in these veins."

Liam mimed wiping sweat from his brow and then offered Lily his arm. "Well then, might I offer my services in showing you around the games today? Perhaps I can even convince you to cheer me on in the caber toss later this afternoon."

Lily took his arm with a broad smile. She couldn't have asked for a better introduction to the games than to be shown around by one of the competitors. "I'd be happy to have you as my guide today. The caber toss was already on my list of events to see, and I think I just might be able to send a few shouts your way."

Liam smiled and turned back to the dancing still taking place on the stage in front of them. "Let me begin by telling you a little more about this dancing then," Liam began.

Lily listened happily as Liam described the different dance moves, their origins, and the way the judges scored the competition. They spent some more time watching the dancing and then began moving around the grounds to other competitions. His knowledge of both the history and details of the events made him easy to listen to.

Liam also proved to be quite the flirt as he escorted Lily around the games that day. He constantly begged to be touching her, claiming she was his lucky charm. Whether it was offering his arm, guiding her with a hand on her back, or just claiming her hand completely, he never wanted to be very far away from Lily. His smiles in her direction didn't hurt either. Lily noticed that he watched her reactions constantly and seemed pleased by her enthusiasm for the games.

When they made their way to the caber toss that afternoon, Lily understood for the first time just how strong someone had to be in order to participate. The goal of the caber toss was to literally throw a tree. Liam explained the finer points for Lily as she stood in awe of the men hoisting their heavy loads. The athlete had to lift a tree vertically, holding the smaller end in his hands. He then had to toss it so that the upper end would rotate around and strike the ground first. The goal with the smaller end was to have it hit the ground in a twelve-o'clock position from the direction of the athlete's run. If he was successful, then it was said that the he'd turned the caber.

Liam finished his explanation then bowed over Lily's hand and offered it a quick kiss. "I'm off to battle, lass. Wish me luck."

He tossed a wink in her direction, and she waved as he walked off toward the waiting area for the competitors. A short time later, Lily watched as he took his place at the start and prepared to throw his caber. He looked over at her with a smile right before beginning his try. She returned his grin and then found herself holding her breath and silently sending good vibes his way.

Liam grunted as he lifted his heavy load, made his run, and succeeded in turning the caber. Lily cheered as loudly as the rest of the crowd in seeing a successful try, and Liam was all grins when he came back over to her side. He picked her up, turned her in a circle, and gave her a huge hug. "I knew you'd be a lucky one the moment I saw you. Now, I just have to convince you to stick with me for the rest of the competition, and I'm sure to win."

Lily laughed at his enthusiasm and graciously accepted his invitation to remain with him while she was at the games. Yes, indeed, she was very glad that she had decided to come to Scotland.

35
chapter

Ammon stood on Lily's front porch talking himself into knocking on the door. Her car sat in the driveway and he thought he saw the glow of a light through the window slats, so he figured she was home. He really should knock before she looked out the window and caught him standing there, but he found himself hesitating. His hands were shaking, and his breathing was unsteady. He felt more right now than he had in months. Excitement, nervousness, hope, and anticipation all fought for room in his heart.

It had taken him the better part of a year to realize just how much he was allowing fear to ruin his life. The fear of repeating the past, of opening his heart again, and of not being enough for someone else had taken him away from the one person he truly loved. He had run away from Lily instead of working through his insecurities with her and, in doing so, he had lost the most precious thing in his life.

The conversation with his mother had repeated in his head over and over until he finally realized she was right. His pride wouldn't let him admit he still had a lot to give, even if Laura had initially rejected him. He had marginalized his own good points until all he saw were faults. Somehow, Lily had seen past his self-depreciation and into his heart. She'd found the good and fallen in love with him, despite his efforts to push her away.

Lily deserved better than how he'd treated her. He had loved her but still left without any regard to her feelings or needs. He didn't deserve her love or her loyalty, but he heartily wished that she would allow him to win her back. He'd spent sixteen months of his life being away from Lily, and he wasn't going to waste any more. All his feelings for her consumed him, and yesterday he'd gotten in his car and started driving back to Utah after finishing his latest shoot in New Mexico. The miles had flown by as he thought only of coming back here to Lily. He only hoped he wasn't too late.

He finally knocked and then waited with bated breath. However, no footsteps sounded from the other side of the door. Ammon knew it was late enough in the day that Lily wouldn't be sleeping. He knocked again, just in case she hadn't heard him the first time. Again, no response. Some of the nervousness left, and Ammon started thinking about where she might be. It was a hot afternoon to go for a run, but maybe she had decided to do a workout at the gym. He walked down the porch steps and stretched out in the grass under the shadow of her oak tree. He would wait. He would wait forever if it meant he would have another chance with Lily.

Slowly, the afternoon stretched into evening, and there was still no sign of Lily. Even if she'd gone for a long run, she should be home by now. He hadn't left her front lawn since he'd arrived, so he knew he hadn't missed her going inside either.

Ammon rubbed his face while walking to his car and thought through his options. If he really wanted to find Lily, he knew where he needed to go, but he wasn't looking forward to it. He wasn't sure if he would even be given the information he so desperately craved, but his need to find Lily outweighed his dread. Ammon took a deep breath, turned on his car, and headed down the road.

It was time to talk to Will.

*****

Will opened the door, and Ammon saw his face immediately go hard. He didn't say anything; he just stared at Ammon with cold, angry eyes. Ammon hadn't spoken to Will since he'd left Utah over a year ago, and Will hadn't reached out to contact him either. Will probably hated him, and he wouldn't blame him because he hated himself.

Ammon took a deep breath and said the only thing he could. "I'm so sorry, Will."

Will stared at him for a few moments longer then, crossing his arms over his chest, replied, "I'm not the one you should be saying that to."

"I know," Ammon rushed to say, "but I don't know where she is. I need your help to find her. It's taken me so long to figure out how wrong I was. I don't want to waste another moment before trying to set things right."

Will looked at him appraisingly, then opened the door and motioned him inside. "You're lucky Kate's not home. She'd probably tear you limb from limb."

"It would be no more than I deserve. I thought that was your job though," Ammon replied.

"My job is to act tough so that people know Lily's being watched over. Kate is the one that would actually do the deed. Though she might ask me to hold her victims down for her while she dismembered them."

Ammon smiled slightly at the mental picture but quickly became serious again. "I meant what I said, Will. I owe Lily a thousand apologies and more. I treated her poorly, and she was worthy of so much better. I don't deserve her, but I need her to know that I love her. Even if she can never trust me again, even if she no longer wants me in her life. I need her to know how I felt about her. How I still feel about her."

"What if she's moved on? What if she's with someone else and your declaration will just cast a shadow over what she's built?"

Ammon gulped. That was his worst fear: that he'd waited too long and that she was no longer within his reach to even express his feelings to. He didn't want to ask, but he had to know. "Has she moved on, Will? Is she seeing someone else? Have I missed my chance?"

Will stood in the front room, contemplating Ammon. Ammon knew that his future rested in Will's hands right now. His entire body tensed, waiting for Will's answer.

"She's not seeing anyone else."

Ammon took a deep breath, feeling relieved. At least there was still a chance. "Do you know where she is? Is she out with Kate?"

"She's in Scotland."

At first, Ammon didn't understand. But then his brain finally processed Will's answer. "Scotland? Why's she there? She's not there permanently, is she?"

"No. She went on a vacation to visit Jack and see some of the sights. She went by herself, which I don't love, but it's not like I can stop her. She at least gave Jack her rough itinerary so we'd know which area she'd be in most of the time."

"Scotland," Ammon said softly to himself. He took a deep breath and looked imploringly at Will. "Would you be willing to give me a copy of her itinerary?"

Will looked surprised. "You're not thinking of going over there to see her, are you?"

"I am," Ammon answered, working out the logistics in his head even as he talked with Will. "I have frequent flyer miles that I need to use. But even if I didn't, I meant what I said. I'm not wasting another minute. I need Lily to know how I feel, and I need to know if she could ever forgive me."

Will stared at Ammon for a few moments, looking pensive. "Well, if you're that serious about it, then I guess you really have changed. Let me see if she gave a copy to Kate before she left."

"Thanks," Ammon said distractedly as Will walked toward his bedroom. He mentally ran through a checklist of everything he would have to get done before he got on the plane. He was sure that he could be ready to fly by tomorrow morning, though his departure would depend on the airline's schedule.

His excitement at seeing Lily increased. If he was lucky, he might be with her within the next forty-eight hours. He prayed that things would work out to get him over there and that Lily would want to hear what he so desperately wanted to say.

36
chapter

Lily enjoyed the rest of the time she spent with Liam while at the games. Even though he was a huge flirt, Liam proved to be a perfect gentleman and never pushed her beyond a comfortable friendship. In fact, she got so used to Liam holding her hand that she started to miss his warmth when he wasn't there. She never thought she'd get to the point where she could think of someone else without constantly comparing him with Ammon. Liam was so different, though, and her experiences in Scotland so removed from her life back home that she found it easy to focus on just being with him.

She enjoyed all the different activities they did together. They tried several pubs in the area around where the games took place, looking for new favorite foods. Lily loved the potato leek soup she had one night, while Liam generally stuck to more meat-based dishes. Though she didn't drink, she loved being in the pubs and watching the different people interact there. It was easy to pick out the regulars. She enjoyed seeing them come together and greet their friends as they shared stories about their days.

Though Liam lived in Inverness, there were enough people in town for the games that Lily felt like she met most of his friends from back home. No matter where they went, someone always knew Liam. Lily happily watched his interactions with his friends while they ate; they were an entertaining lot. Liam always tried to include Lily in their conversations too, and she felt like she learned more about Scotland from those dinners than she ever had before.

She thought about him now as she drove back across the country. It had been an amazing three days getting to know Liam. He proved to be kind, thoughtful, obviously strong but also gentle in his mannerisms. Lily knew she was attracted to him, and she knew he would be open to seeing more of her if she gave him a chance.

She was too much of a realist, though. She didn't live in Scotland, and a long-distance relationship, especially across the ocean, would probably not work out well. Still, it had been nice to be noticed. Liam's parting words did give her something to think about, however.

"If you ever decide you're tired of being a colonist, come home to Scotland. Come and spend some more time with me. I think I could convince you that America pales in comparison with the beauty of the highlands. Plus, I'm here. What more do you need?"

Lily had laughed at his self-assurance and promised that she would think about it. Now she wondered, should she seriously consider moving? She would never move just for Liam, though he was a nice bonus if she did decide to come and take up residence in Scotland. She did love the country. The history, the beauty, and the people all fit her personality. Maybe she should look into it. Besides, Jack was over here and probably would be for a while, so she would even be close to part of her family.

Her parents wouldn't love it, and she would miss Kate and Will too. However, this trip had awakened her spirit of wanderlust. A move here didn't have to be permanent. She could always go back to the States if she wanted to. She thought about her friends who did travel nursing. They loved the opportunity to see new places and meet new people. This would be different, obviously, but the idea behind it was the same. She felt like she needed a change. A chance to explore the new person she'd become without her comfortable surroundings. As much as she loved her house and the area where she lived, there were too many memories there to completely look toward the future.

Her brain continued to weigh the pros and cons of her options as she drove. At first, she intended to drive straight back to Edinburgh after the games. She only had a few days left in Scotland and wanted to spend some more time with Jack, but as she neared Glasgow, she noticed the turn off for the road to Perth. She knew if she took the northbound road, she would eventually connect in with the road to Stonehaven. Dunnottar Castle was in Stonehaven.

She longed to see the castle before she left Scotland. Her last visit there had been so euphoric, and she wanted to capture that feeling again. Maybe being back in that familiar location would help her sort out her thoughts about coming to Scotland more permanently.

Lily took the road heading north. Jack wouldn't care that she changed her plans, but she would send him a message the next time she stopped for fuel just so he wouldn't worry. She knew there was a small inn near the castle too; it was where she had stayed last time. She hoped it would have an opening tonight, because she would reach Stonehaven too late to get into the castle.

Tomorrow was the day then. She would take her time and wander the grounds, allowing the castle to work its magic. Surely, the peace she felt there would help calm her turbulent feelings. She looked forward to working through her thoughts and deciding what would be the best course for her future.

37
chapter

Ammon's flight landed at the Edinburgh Airport early in the morning. He had tried to sleep on the overnight flight, but his rest was fitful at best. He kept thinking about what he would say to Lily to adequately convey his feelings for her. Nothing seemed quite right.

He made it to the car rental desk and soon found himself on the road toward Jack's apartment, Will having given him the address along with Lily's itinerary. According to Lily's schedule, she should have returned to Edinburgh yesterday. He knew she wouldn't be sleeping at Jack's, but he hoped he would catch her there for a late breakfast. If nothing else, at least Jack could tell him where she was.

He felt invigorated being in the same country as Lily. He hoped she would be happy to see him, although he knew she would be surprised. No doubt she wrote him off a long time ago. Will had said that she wasn't seeing anyone else that he knew of, though, so that reassured Ammon that he might still have a chance.

His GPS dinged to tell him he had arrived at his destination. Unlike his hesitation on Lily's porch, Ammon's anxious desire to see Lily outweighed any nervousness he felt. He leapt from the car and quickly made his way up to Jack's apartment. He knocked and waited impatiently. After only a moment, Jack himself unlocked the latch and opened the door. "Ammon," he said, looking wary.

"Jack, hi. Is Lily here?"

Jack looked him up and down, and Ammon sensed that Lily had another protector in her younger brother.

"Did Will tell you I was coming?"

"He sent me a message. I just wasn't sure you'd actually show up," Jack replied coolly.

"I messed up, Jack. I hurt her, and I'm so sorry. But I'm trying to make it up to her. I just need to find her and talk to her."

Ammon hoped that Jack would trust him enough to tell him where Lily was. He supposed he could wait in his car for her to show up here, but he didn't know how long that would take.

"She's not here right now," Jack finally responded.

"Is she at your friend's house still? Could you give me her address?"

"No. I meant she's not back in Edinburgh yet. She decided to go visit one more castle before she came back to the city."

Ammon had a sudden suspicion about where Lily might be. "Is she at Dunnottar?"

Jack looked surprised. Perhaps he didn't think Ammon really knew Lily well enough to guess where she'd be. But Ammon did know Lily. He knew her better than he knew anyone else in the world, and he knew what that place meant to her. The only thing she didn't know was how much it meant to him as well.

"Yes, she's there. She's coming back tonight, though, if you want to wait."

"I can't wait," Ammon replied, already turning to leave. "I've waited too long already."

*****

Lily wandered the grounds of the castle feeling soothed. There were so many castles in Europe, but none of them spoke to her like this one did. Something about the majesty of this fortress on the ocean made her feel at peace. She walked through all the old buildings, revisiting the sites she'd seen years ago. The plaques describing the areas of the castle were the same, though Lily read them again just to jog her memory.

Lily felt a lot like this castle. The storms of life and the oceans of despair she had endured had threatened to knock her down. But just like these old buildings, she continued to stand, and she discovered that she was stronger than she thought she was. In her own way, she felt just as majestic as the buildings she'd just seen. Weathered, perhaps, but still reaching toward the sky. For a moment she fingered the necklace Trixie had given her. She was trying to reach for the stars, just as Trixie wanted her to.

But she still needed to make a decision about the next step on her life's journey. She wanted a place to think without anyone else around. She looked around the grounds, trying to find a quiet area. She found herself walking toward the old sentry box positioned at the corner of the castle. The view looked out onto the ocean, and Lily had discovered last time that it was her favorite spot to sit and think. Fewer people came out toward this end of the castle, opting to stay closer to the main buildings.

The crowds weren't too bad today. A brief morning shower must have scared away a few of them, but Lily loved how it cooled the warm summer air. She still wore a light sweater to protect herself from the sun and the ocean breeze, but she felt perfectly comfortable.

She arrived at her chosen spot and stood near the wall that separated her from the drop to the cliffs below. Her thoughts were still restless. She'd spent all morning thinking about the idea of moving to Scotland. There were so many positives about the idea, but for some reason it didn't feel quite right, and she couldn't figure out why. So she had decided to come and let the ocean speak to her. It would help her decide what to do.

The small crowds thinned even further as most people left the grounds to find lunch in the nearby village. Lily had enjoyed a large Scottish breakfast and still felt full, and she was happy she didn't feel the need to leave to go find food. Instead, she settled herself into a comfortable place along the wall and rested her arms on the rough stones. She closed her eyes and just listened. The answer would come.

38

chapter

Ammon's nerves increased as he drove the route to the castle. He hoped he could find Lily there. He knew that his words and her reaction would define the rest of his life.

He pulled into the parking lot just after noon and quickly walked the inclined path up to the gatehouse and onto the grounds. The memories of being here before assailed him. He vividly recalled how it felt to see Lily here the last time. He had never told her about it; it was such a precious memory. The picture he took of her on that occasion still rested in his wallet, and he smiled at the irony. He'd come to Dunnottar that day to take a picture of the castle. Instead, he saw Lily, and that simple encounter had changed his life.

He looked around at the castle, but this time his eyes weren't imagining angles and light. This time he came in search of the woman from his picture. Her beauty had caught his eye all those years ago, but then her personality and spirit had captured his heart in a way no static scene ever could.

Ammon began walking through the buildings, his eyes continuously roving over the sparse crowds looking for her familiar face. A futile search of the structures proved Lily was not anywhere inside. Ammon looked toward the old sentry box. She couldn't be there. It would be too much of a coincidence. Instinctively, his feet turned toward the path that would lead him to the exact spot where he'd first seen Lily. His heart pounded as he grew closer, and it became difficult to breathe.

He rounded a corner and found her in the same position he had first seen her. The clothes were different, but the feeling was the same. Her eyes were closed, her body leaning toward the ocean. The light wind still played with her hair, and her face once again radiated a glow Ammon associated only with Lily.

His feet kept moving, though his brain seemed to have stopped working. He walked until he stood just a few feet behind her. She must have been completely absorbed in her thoughts, because she did not turn and acknowledge his presence.

He stood there for a few moments, taking in the sight of Lily. How he loved her. He sent up a prayer that this wouldn't be the last time he got to be near her. He opened his mouth to say something, but nothing would come out. He didn't know how to start. He couldn't find the right words to express everything he felt. Finally, he was able to form a word. Just one word.

"Lily."

*****

Lily froze, the breath caught in her throat. She knew that voice. Her eyes snapped open as a rush of memories flashed through her mind. Joy, love, pain, and sorrow—each emotion found a place within her heart, until at last she settled into something that felt like peace. Even though she thought she would never see him again, she knew, like she knew the sun would rise in the morning, that she still loved the man with that voice. She released the air caught in her lungs and slowly turned around.

Ammon stood there, his arms slightly outstretched, as he stared at her. One of the first things she noticed were his eyes. The eyes looking at her were no longer haunted. Instead, they looked anxious and hopeful. The heavy burden of doubt seemed lifted, replaced by the uncertainty he must feel about her reaction to seeing him again.

What would her reaction be? she wondered. He'd left her so long ago it seemed. She knew she still loved him, but she was different now. She loved herself as well, and no longer would she feel only gratitude for a man's admiration. She knew she was worth being loved as much as she would love back.

She thought about everything that had happened since she met Ammon. She would not deny that she still wanted him in her life, but she needed to know that he'd truly changed and wanted her too. If that was even the reason he was here. This could all just be a strange coincidence. Perhaps, his work had sent him here, and he stumbled on her by accident. She needed to know.

"Ammon." Lily paused and then decided to be forthright. "Why are you here?"

"I'm here for you, Lily." His words came out in a rush as if he wanted to share everything in his heart quickly before she could turn him away. "I should have come back to you ages ago. In fact, I never should have left. I love you. I've loved you from the moment I first saw you, even if I didn't know you. You're the only person I want to be with. I'm not always good with words, but I want you to know that I'm here to stay. I want to regain your trust, and I want to win back your love. I want to be yours, if you'll have me."

Lily felt overwhelmed by his declaration. Her mind latched onto one of the things he said, and she asked, "What do you mean you loved me before you knew me? The first time I met you was at my house for dinner. You were kind, but I wouldn't say you loved me."

Ammon looked at her for a moment and then slowly pulled out his wallet. Lily found herself curious to know what he was looking for. What would be in his wallet that had to do with answering her question? She creased her eyebrows as he pulled out an obviously worn photograph. He held it in his hands and stared at the image for a moment. Then, slowly, he raised his eyes to her as he handed her the photograph. Lily watched him for a moment before glancing down at the picture.

She gasped as she fought to comprehend what this was. She recognized herself, but she was here at Dunnottar. This was the trip she'd taken years ago. How had Ammon come by this picture of her? She'd been here by herself, so she knew she didn't have any personal photos taken from a distance. Plus, she rarely put herself in her pictures anyway. She preferred landscapes to selfies. She looked at him in astonishment, and she could tell he understood her silent question.

"I was here at the same time you were all those years ago. I didn't know who you were, but when I saw you, I was struck with your beauty. It wasn't just your outward appearance, though you are very attractive. I could see in you a serenity that I lacked. It was completely alluring. It still is. I fell in love with the girl I took a picture of. And then I fell in love with you in real life."

"Why didn't you ever tell me?" Lily whispered, still shocked at his revelation.

"At first, I didn't want you to think that I was some kind of crazy stalker. It's insane that I even met you in person. Of all the people on all the days I've been here, *you* were the only one that ever stuck out. Then, after I started seeing you, I came to love you for who you are, not just as the girl at the castle. In time, the real you replaced the thought of the woman in the photograph so completely that I didn't want to lessen what we had by comparing my memory with the real you. I hope you can forgive me."

Lily nodded slowly. "I'm flattered that you saw something in me that I didn't even know was there. After you left," she paused, then gathering her courage, she continued on, "I broke. I'd put so much of myself into being with you that I'd lost sight of who I was without you. And it wasn't just you. I never saw myself as having worth much at all, especially as far as men were concerned."

Ammon looked ready to interrupt, but Lily raised a hand to stop him. She needed him to listen and understand what she was about to say. "I want to say thank you," she continued, and Ammon's face changed to a look of surprise. "Granted, I feel like I could have gone an entire lifetime without feeling the despair I felt when you left. But because of it, I was able to finally see that I wasn't being fair to myself. I thought I had no worth, because no one ever wanted to be with me. But what I failed to see was that I am enough. Of course, I'll always have room to improve, but I finally see that who I am right now is worth being loved. And that love needed to begin with myself."

Lily felt lightened having shared her discoveries with Ammon. Instead of being ashamed of her struggles, she rejoiced in the changes they wrought in her. If Ammon was truly the man for her, he would find joy in her self-worth too.

"Lily, is it possible that I'm even more in love with you now having heard what you just told me? You've always had worth to me, but knowing that you think so too is one of the most amazingly attractive things I've ever heard. I'm only sorry that I ever gave you reason to doubt yourself. That night you went on your date." Ammon shook his head, then continued. "It made me realize how I felt about you. In fact, I was ready to walk out the door, march straight to your house, and tell you how much I loved you."

Lily felt astonished. At her look of shock, Ammon smiled sadly. "I was halfway to my door, when Laura showed up."

If Lily was shocked before, there were no words to describe how she felt now.

"She came in and began talking to me as if she'd never left. She thought she could waltz right back into my life without a word of apology for her behavior. She thought I'd still want her. That I was still in love with her."

Lily swallowed slowly, some of her earlier fears about coming in second place returning. "And did you want her? Did you still love her?"

"No, Lily." Ammon looked at her imploringly. "I'd fallen completely in love with you. I loved you more than I ever cared for Laura. I hope you believe me when I say the reason I left you wasn't because I didn't love you."

Lily felt relief and then confusion. "If you loved me, then why did you leave?"

Ammon looked ashamed. "Seeing Laura again brought out all my old fears of rejection and mistrust. I already felt like I wasn't good enough for you, and her appearance reminded me just how broken I was. For so long, my first response had been to run, and I let it take over again. It's no excuse. I should have stayed and worked through my problems. I know now that you would have been there for me, but Laura destroyed my ability to trust people. And although I had started to trust you, I still didn't trust myself to be enough. I'm so sorry, Lily."

At last it all made sense, and Lily felt immense relief in finally understanding the entire picture. Though she knew his departure was not her fault, seeing the situation from his point of view helped her know exactly how damaged he'd been and just how far he'd come to be here with her now. Lily began to smile in earnest as her thoughts coalesced into one happy truth. He really did love her.

Ammon looked at her, watching the emotions play across her face. After a moment, he slowly stepped close enough to reach out for her hand. Lily allowed him to take hold of it, and he tenderly brought it close to his heart.

"Lily, will you ever forgive me? I'll wait as long as it takes. I only want to know that sometime in the future, I might hope to have you in my life once more. I'll do whatever you ask to prove that I'm sincere. I don't ever want to leave you again, Lily. Please say that I can stay."

His eyes looked imploringly into hers, and she felt the last of her reservations fade away. She could see that he was serious and that he truly wanted her back. "You can stay," she whispered.

His smile blossomed widely on his face as he pulled her into a tight hug. She felt like he was holding onto her as though she might try and slip away and only the strength of his grip would prevent it. She didn't mind. It had been so long since she felt this way. Being in his arms was like coming home.

"What can I do to earn your forgiveness?" Ammon asked into her hair. His breath tickled her neck, and she shivered in delight. She'd forgotten just how much she enjoyed being held by this man.

"You've earned it already. I was never angry at you," she added, gripping him more tightly. "All I ever wanted was for you to love me back."

"I do love you, Lily," Ammon said, pulling back slightly to look into her eyes as he made his declaration. "I lied that day when I said I didn't. I love you more than I've ever loved anyone."

"I love you too, Ammon."

At her words, he pulled her tightly against him again. He held her there for some time before pulling back to look at her once more.

His eyes searched hers, and she felt a giddy anticipation build up inside her.

"I know it might be too soon, but may I kiss you?"

Lily wanted nothing more. She nodded, and he lowered his head toward her. His lips caught hers in the most tender kiss she'd ever experienced. Gradually he deepened it until it seemed as though she could no longer tell where she stopped and he began.

Eventually, Ammon drew back and placed his forehead against hers. His hands found her face, and he cupped her cheeks tenderly, caressing them with his thumbs. "I love you," he repeated. Before she could respond, he leaned toward her again. Her soul took flight as his lips once again captured hers. Far below, she could hear the sound of the waves crashing against the cliffs, echoing the fierce beating of her heart.

EPILOGUE

One year later

Lily and Ammon both sighed in relief at the same time then looked at each other and laughed. They had finally left their reception behind, and the quiet of Ammon's car felt relaxing after a full day of socializing.

Not that she would change a thing about it, Lily thought as she looked down at her left hand. Ammon's right hand gripped it tightly, but she could still see the sparkle from her ring glistening in the light of passing street lamps. She could hardly believe it was real. Ammon was hers forever, and she was his. The thought excited her, and she glanced at Ammon, only to find him returning her look. The anticipation of a life together gave her a heady feeling.

"I'm glad Will finally gave his permission for me to marry you," Ammon joked after a moment. "I wasn't sure he was going to for a while."

Lily chuckled, thinking about her older brother. Will's protective instincts had been in full force when she had returned from Scotland with Ammon. It took Ammon months of consistent good behavior for him to regain Will's trust and then blessing for their relationship.

The rest of her family took their lead from Lily. She forgave Ammon completely, and so they followed by welcoming him without question. His family welcomed her gladly as well, and Lily felt happy to be surrounded by such love. Now, as she looked over at Ammon again and saw his smile, she knew that her joy was complete. Their journey had not been easy, but, looking back, Lily decided that it had all been worth it.

Ammon finished the short drive from the reception venue to Lily's house. Their house, she mentally corrected herself. Ammon unbuckled himself and, with a gesture to stay still, quickly rose from his side of the car and came to her door. He gallantly opened it, took Lily's hand to help her emerge from her seat, then swept her off her feet.

Lily laughed as Ammon carried her to the front door. She held his shoulders tightly as he loosened his grip to let them inside. He carried her across the threshold and closed the door with his foot.

Lily's laughter faded as she looked into his eyes. The once-shuttered expression now appeared alight with joy, the brilliant blueness filled with love and longing. Lily's breath caught as she returned his gaze with one of her own, equally alive with hope and promise for the future.

Ammon's face leaned toward her, and his mouth gently caught hers in a loving caress. A fire lit inside her as their embrace continued, and Lily knew, without a doubt, that this was where she belonged.

BOOK CLUB DISCUSSION QUESTIONS

1. Have you ever found yourself disbelieving or dismissing compliments given to you by others? Do you think society encourages us to belittle our talents? Why?
2. Lily questions her worth because she is single. She allows herself to be defined by something she thinks she lacks. What are we using to define ourselves?
3. Ammon initially chooses to run away instead of facing his fears. What fears are causing us to miss out on experiences that could lead to happiness?
4. Lily chooses not to be angry at Ammon, even though his actions hurt her. Do you think that her forgiveness allowed her to eventually show forgiveness to herself? How difficult is it to truly forgive the ones who hurt us the most?
5. Lily's family and friends helped her when she felt depressed and discouraged. Who do we know that is struggling with these feelings? What are good ways to show love without dismissing the validity of their feelings?

FREEING TRIXIE

Excited green eyes looked out at the snow as the subway car sped down the tracks toward downtown Washington DC during its above-ground section of the route. The early December storm came with enough force to coat the ground in several inches of white powder, and Trixie smiled at the beauty it created. From her vantage point, she could look out at the buildings of Catholic University as the train began to slow in preparation to stop at the Brookland-CUA station.

She still had several stations to go before she would disembark, so Trixie leaned back in her seat and allowed her mind to drift. Though many would have closed their eyes and napped through the journey, Trixie's state of constant vigilance would not allow for such indulgence. In fact, she couldn't remember the last time she'd completely relaxed. Even at home, she constantly checked locks, looked out her windows, and paid attention to the sounds her house made. She wanted to be familiar with its normal noises so that she could sense a change that could warn her of danger.

Most people didn't have to live in this state of hyperawareness, but Trixie felt it to be not only necessary but vital to her survival. She tried to do everything she could to ensure her own safety since there was no one else she could trust to keep her out of harm's way. Even the metro posed a risk, though Trixie deemed it to be a lower risk, and thus, she chanced the journey once a month to visit a museum or a national monument. She loved history and couldn't let the opportunity pass to see more of the nation's rich heritage up-close.

Happy with her museum experience for the day, Trixie walked back out to the entrance, once again watching the people around her for any reactions to her movements. Noting none, she walked out onto the mall and looked around. The sun was setting, and the sky had cleared enough that she could see the pinks and oranges of a beautiful sunset. The lights were turning on as well, and Trixie knew that soon the entire mall area would cast a glowing beacon of light into the night. With the addition of Christmas lights strung in different areas around the White House and the Sculpture Garden, it truly felt like a winter wonderland.

It was toward this second location that Trixie now turned her feet. She pulled a sandwich out of her bag and munched on it as she crossed the paths from the Air and Space Museum to the outdoor ice rink contained within the grounds of the National Gallery of Art Sculpture Garden area. The air felt crisp but not too cold yet. This next activity was to be her second indulgence of the day. Normally, she headed home before the night fell, but she felt like spoiling herself with a few laps around the ice rink. She'd grown up ice-skating, though she never wanted to do it professionally. Still, the feel of the smooth ice beneath her feet as she flew through the open air brought back sweet remembrances from her childhood, and for a moment she decided she could let go of her constant anxiety and just enjoy life.

Not wanting to lug her skates with her all day, she'd left her own pair at home and had to rent from the rink. After pulling her dark brown hair into a bun, she shoved her bag and shoes into a locker and then took to the ice. The sun was completely set now, and the glow of the lights around the rink, along with the Christmas lights hanging in the trees around her, made the world feel magical.

Trixie made unhurried laps around the rink. Over the gates and walls of the garden, she could see some of the museums illuminated with lights. There was a special feeling, she decided, being in the center of DC. The history lived in the streets, and she loved feeling connected with the past. She thought about extending her visit even longer by walking down toward the Washington Monument before she headed back to the subway but then realized it would add another hour or so to her day and she still had to drive home.

The other skaters began departing the ice, and Trixie realized it was time for the Zamboni to do its hourly re-icing. With a contented sigh, she left the ice. Though her ticket said she could stay for one more session of skating, she decided to start her journey home.

She walked over to her locker and removed her belongings before bending down to untie her skates. Once she pulled them off, she looked up out of habit and took a quick glance at her surroundings. She'd relaxed during her adventures today, though the feelings of anxiety never entirely abated, and felt almost calm for the first time in months.

She was about to return her attention to her shoes when suddenly she caught sight of a profile in the crowd that brought an instant return of fear to her heart. Her breathing became shallow and fast, her hands began to sweat, and she could feel the adrenaline coursing through her body. For a moment she froze, like a deer caught in the headlights, then her muscles tensed as she prepared to make an all-out sprint away from the arena.

ABOUT THE AUTHOR

Originally from Arizona, Jennifer Smith Widmer graduated from Brigham Young University with a bachelor's in nursing and spent most of her time before children as a high-risk labor and delivery nurse in Utah and Maryland. She ended up marrying a farmer and moved to rural eastern Idaho.

Lately, her life consists of running around after an energetic three-year-old girl and busy one-year-old twin boys. In her spare time (wait, what's that?), she tries to garden in the high mountain desert, hike and rock climb when she can, and stargaze.

CPSIA information can be obtained
at www.ICGtesting.com
Printed in the USA
BVHW081134250621
610447BV00003B/413